20 April 2002

To Nancy,

I feel blessed.

friendship.

Love,
Deborah

The
Reluctant
Psychic

The Reluctant Psychic

Deborah Heinecker

To order additional copies of this book, contact:
Xlibris Corporation
1-888-7-XLIBRIS
www.Xlibris.com
Orders@Xlibris.com

Contents

This book is for my husband, Bob Wickless,
and in loving memory of my Dad, Calvin (Babe) Heinecker,
my Mom, Lorraine Heinecker,
and my Maternal Grandparents, George and Evelyn Allers.

Author's Note

This mystery is a fictionalized account of my transformation from successful businesswoman to reluctant psychic detective.

As I have worked on cases, I have been privy to personal information about victims, their respective families and acquaintances. I have seen the anguish on family members' faces and heard their tearful pleas for closure.

I believe those people have a right to their privacy and to be spared a tell-all book describing their ordeal.

Therefore, I have totally altered each case including the actual events in order to save those personally involved from any additional pain. Any resemblance to actual events or persons, living or dead, is entirely coincidental.

Acknowledgments

I would like to thank the following:

Bob Wickless, my husband, for encouraging me to write, affording me the opportunity, and editing my manuscript.

Jacqueline and Justin Tucker, and Rick Kendricks, Civil War Re-enactors, who are members of the 93rd Pennsylvania Volunteer Infantry from Lebanon, Pennsylvania, for providing the information about Civil War era dress, customs and re-enactments.

William Sellers, Rescue Chief, and Kim Sellers, EMT and Treasurer, of the Blue Ridge Mountain Fire and Rescue Company for providing the information about fires, and emergency medical procedures.

Becky Dietrich for editing my manuscript and painting the watercolor landscape used on the cover.

Shauna Ansel for providing all aspects of my author's photograph.

Susan Hart for creating my personal website.

Ann Miller Ogaitis, my fourth and fifth grade teacher, for introducing me to the French language, Rimsky-Korsakoff's *Scheherazade*, and creative writing. She encouraged all of her students to explore their talents. She is the quintessential educator.

Alexandra Rymland, my mentor through many incarnations, for helping me to realize that I am a self-actualizing woman.

Gary Kubala, VMD, for your help.

Chapter 1

"I'm not a psychic," I insisted. "I'm a Certified Public Accountant."

"Miss St. George didn't you just finish telling Sgt. Lawrence and me you sometimes see visions of events that have happened in the past or are about to happen in the future?" Commander Herschel replied in an authoritative voice.

"Yes."

"Then for my money, you are a psychic," the Commander concluded.

*　　*　　*

I remember how embarrassed I was to admit to those two police officers that I was psychic. While I believe everyone has psychic abilities, most people refuse to acknowledge them. Many people shun responsibility—especially the responsibility for their own futures. They would rather pay someone else to define their destinies for them. And the person providing that definition, be it psychic, palm reader or psychiatrist, is then blamed when their client is unhappy with his or her life.

I remember the summer I was forced to redefine my

destiny. My aspiration after college to become a partner in an old-line accounting firm had been all encompassing. I ultimately achieved my goal, but found myself resenting my long hours in the office while my staff and what seemed like the rest of the world enjoyed their lives. I began to question my choices.

*   *   *

The date was July 29, 1998. Baltimore was experiencing a typical summer. Temperatures and relative humidity were holding at 95. The window air conditioners in my stone and stucco cottage provided little relief from the heat and dampness typical of an old home in Oak Forest near the Patapsco River.

I rose early. I fed and performed latrine duty for my animal companions, 13 cats and 4 dogs. All strays or rejects.

It was Sunday, and I could afford the time to eat breakfast instead of rushing out the door with suit jacket and briefcase in hand. I relaxed at the kitchen table and savored my Irish Breakfast tea and English muffin with lemon conserve. As I scanned the morning paper, a brief article in *The Sun*'s main section caught my attention. "LOST POLICE DOG," the title read. My affinity for animals made this story more compelling than the paper's lead story about a drug-related homicide in Baltimore City. The article reported a German Shepherd, a member of the Lennoxville Police Department's K-9 Division, had broken his lead and run away from his handler. The article stated the dog had been missing for three days, described the dog as unapproachable due to his training, included the Lennoxville Police Department's telephone number, and asked anyone seeing him to report his location to them immediately.

Veiled images filtered into my mind. I envisioned a German Shepherd chasing a rabbit across a field, his broken lead trailing behind him. A striking moon illuminated his movements. The dog chased the rabbit into a heavily wooded area. The rabbit scurried along the bank of a shallow stream. The dog slowed his pace as he approached a fallen tree blocking his path. He jumped over the trunk and continued running toward the stream, but the end of his long lead became snagged on the tree. Suddenly, his head jerked backward, and he flipped onto his side. His chest heaved as he gulped for air. The dog eventually raised himself onto his front legs and shook his head like a stunned boxer attempting to clear his mind. He lunged toward the stream, but his taut lead held fast. The dog could not reach the water. He continued to pant. He eventually laid down on the stream bank and rested his chin on his paws.

I pushed my breakfast away. My second-story cat, Ariel, promptly jumped onto the kitchen table and stole my English muffin. I was too upset to care. I worried that the missing German Shepherd was hungry, thirsty or hurt. I paced around my kitchen wondering how I could help that dog. The grandfather clock in the hallway struck ten thirty. I had a tennis match scheduled for noon, but that seemed unimportant. I dialed my tennis partner's number to cancel, let it ring once then hung up. Had I lost my mind? What made me think my vision was of the lost police dog? That German Shepherd could have been one I saw yesterday, last week, last year. Perhaps my imagination was overactive. That would have been my mother's explanation.

I had always had experiences that could have been described as psychic; however, I rarely shared those experiences with anyone outside my immediate family. My mother would have been furious if she thought I had said or done anything to undermine our family's stellar reputation.

I redialed my tennis partner, Ric's, number. If I considered anyone my best friend, it was Ric. I knew I could discuss my quandary with him.

"Did you see the article in *The Sun* this morning about

the missing police dog?" I pointed to the newspaper article lying on the kitchen table as if Ric could see it through the receiver.

"Good morning to you, too, Katherine," Ric replied in his typical nonchalant manner. "Yes, I did read the article."

"I have seen that German Shepherd."

"What do you mean? Where have you seen the dog? Incidentally, why aren't you en route to our tennis match? You live farther from the club than I."

"Forget tennis." I took a deep breath and mustered the courage to say, "Ric, you probably will not believe this, but I have seen what I believe to be that police dog." I paused. "The problem is I have seen him in my mind."

"In your mind? In your mind?" Ric's voice grew uncharacteristically loud. "You know, you're doing it again."

"Doing *what* again?" I knew exactly what Ric meant.

"Remember our trip to the cemetery last Christmas?"

"Yes," I said, recalling my usual holiday visit to my family's graves.

"This sounds a bit like that to me. And what exactly will you tell the police, Katherine? That you think you saw their dog, but you can't be sure because you saw the dog only in your mind?" I knew Ric had to be shaking his head in disbelief. "My brother-in-law is a state trooper, remember? This sort of thing is diametrically opposed to everything the police believe. They are taught to work with facts not visions."

Ric's comments made me pause. He was right. The Lennoxville Police would probably hang up on me after I explained how I came by my information. On the off chance that they listened to me, but I failed to find their dog, I would have made a fool of myself. I wondered if I should chance that.

"Katherine are you there?"

"I am aware this sounds ridiculous," I said, my voice strangely unsteady. "I have no reason to believe this, but I feel I can find that police dog." I was overcome with the urge to cry. With my tears came the words, "I must try to find that police dog!"

Ric knew I was not a crier. To the contrary, he had witnessed my shoring up my all is well facade whenever anyone else would have been sobbing in their hankies.

"Katherine, I am not trying to dissuade you, but like it or not police work is based on facts. Face it, that's not what you can offer. However, if they are desperate, they might try anything. Do what you think, no feel, is right. I'm sure you will anyway."

My silence prompted Ric to continue, "I'll cancel our match. Call me if you want to talk later. Good luck, Katherine."

I stared at the article for a long time trying to decide what to do. I finally dialed the number for the Lennoxville Police.

"Lennoxville Police, Sgt. Gurski."

I cleared my throat and said, "I know you are going to think I'm crazy, but I might be able to help you find your missing police dog."

Instead of the expected laughter, Sgt. Gurski replied, "Let me put you through to K-9 Division Commander Herschel. One minute please."

I breathed a sigh of relief at clearing what I perceived as my first hurdle. Commander Herschel answered and I repeated, "I know you are going to think I'm crazy, but I might be able to help you find your missing police dog."

"Miss, I promise I will not think you're crazy. Anything you can do to help us find our dog would be greatly appreciated."

"Perhaps I should explain," I continued tentatively. "I saw a German Shepherd in a wooded area. He was resting on the bank of a stream."

"Then you've seen our dog?"

"Not exactly. I believe I have seen your dog, but I have only seen him in my mind."

Silence.

"That is not as weird as you might think, Commander." I again questioned the propriety of this call. "Often I envision an event which has happened or is about to happen. I have predicted countless . . . ," I began to defend myself, as usual, but chose the offense instead. "The bottom line is my visions are frequently correct."

"I see," Cmdr. Herschel replied. Silence again. I was about to tell him I did not appreciate being patronized when he continued. "Miss, I didn't catch your name."

"You didn't catch it because I haven't given it to you. My name is St. George . . . Katherine St. George."

"Miss St. George, our K-9 is a highly trained and, consequently, very expensive dog. The only vision I need to be correct is the one you have of our missing dog. I, frankly, don't care how we do it as long as we get him back. When can you meet us?"

I was surprised by his candor. I agreed to meet him and the missing dog's handler at two p.m. I hoped that afforded me enough time to shower and attempt to follow the commander's directions to where the dog had been lost.

Afternoon rain was forecast. I wondered if the chill I experienced after my shower was caused by falling temperatures or by my apprehension. Either way, chinos and a long-sleeved polo shirt would suffice. I pulled on my Wellingtons and grabbed my sailing slicker. What would my ex-husband, Colin, have thought of my wandering around in a woods, God knows where, looking for a lost police dog? He would have gladly joined the search.

I recently had begun to realize Colin was not the one I needed to divorce. I needed to divorce myself. Several months ago, I began to feel overly stressed. My mother had insisted I felt guilty for divorcing a man who obviously loved me dearly and would have done anything to make our marriage work. Colin was a successful attorney and a fine person. He and I were the perfect couple. We had a house in Oak Forest filled with antiques and a 30 foot sloop moored in Annapolis. We belonged to the right country clubs. We had everything, or so he thought.

I took a meditation course in order to learn to manage my stress. Meditation became an unexpected avenue for my self-discovery. My life's path became clearer each time I meditated. I realized I was unhappy with my choices, but I feared change. I had stubbornly resisted taking that first step toward a different life. However as I tossed my slicker, purse and directions onto the passenger's seat of my old Volvo station wagon, I knew my search for that police dog would be my seminal step on the new path I needed to follow.

As I drove toward Lennoxville, I remembered Ric's reference to our last trip to the cemetery where my family is buried. I would never forget that day. Even though Ric rarely mentions it I know he wouldn't either.

Snow had fallen several times between Thanksgiving and December 16 last year. Because the 16th was my dad's birthday, I placed Christmas wreaths on dad's and my maternal grandparents' graves on that particular date religiously. Ric offered to drive that day because he knew I still grieved for my dad, and it would be an emotional trip for me. What Ric did not know, and I never mentioned to anyone, was that I still grieved on some level for my long-dead grandparents, my dog, Teddy; my gerbil, Ivy; my canary, Rudolph. Death is the one thing that renders me weak. I suppose that is because death is the one thing I realize I cannot control. All the emotions I manage to suppress day-to-day come gushing to the surface when someone I love, be it animal or person, dies. I feel diminished, deprived, even angry when my loved one dies. Perhaps my mother is right. I am selfish.

The grave markers at Westridge Memorial Park are modern, flat, brass plaques, not the traditional upright headstones I prefer. I suppose those garden-like cemeteries satisfy our uniquely American urge to deny our mortality. Those cemeteries look to the unknowing eye like perfectly manicured fairways. They are golf courses for the departed.

On that particular Sunday, the grave markers were hidden under several layers of snow, and the biting wind had created drifts. As Ric and I drove along the narrow, winding roads to my family graves, Ric looked at the vacant landscape and appeared puzzled. He parked where I directed but hesitated before opening his door. He turned to me as if to say something, but caught himself. Ric shrugged his shoulders and turned away.

"What is it?" I asked.

"I don't mean to bring up the obvious, but this appears to be an empty field," Ric replied, his hand indicating the glacial expanse surrounding us. He shook his head. "How do you propose we find your family's graves? We'll freeze out there with this wind whipping about." Ric noticed the flakes decorating his windshield. "And it's snowing again."

"Don't worry. Just get the wreaths," I answered confidently as I threw open my door allowing an icy blast to penetrate Ric's Saab. I pulled my ski jacket's hood over my head.

Ric got out of his car and hurried to the trunk. I think his quick response reflected more his aversion to winter's fickle weather than his exuberance for our task. Ric flipped up his stadium coat's collar in a futile effort to deflect the wind. His woolen sports car cap provided little protection for his balding head. That was the price he paid for refusing to wear jackets with hoods. Ric turned to me as he opened his trunk. To his surprise, I had marched into the field.

I took about fifteen steps, stopped, then closed my eyes. My back was to Ric as I focused my mind on my dad. I pictured his slender, handsome face and loving hazel eyes. I heard his soft, comforting voice. Guided by an unseen force, I walked slowly through the snow. A feeling of absolute peace embraced me. I tacked right, then left, then right again. I stopped.

I knelt and dug into the snow. I touched a metal surface then slowly brushed the remaining layer of flakes from the plaque. The large, bas relief letters read CHARLES JOHNSTON ST. GEORGE. I sighed. The frigid air stung my throat and lungs. I removed my right glove and touched dad's plaque. My fingers moved lightly across his name etched in the metal. As I rose, tears welled. I called to Ric while blinking back my tears. "Here is Dad. Bring the wreaths." I hoped Ric was too far away to hear the catch in my voice.

We silently placed the wreath on dad's grave. After a few minutes of grave side reflection, I said my goodbye.

I turned to my right, and closed my eyes. I focused my mind on my grandparents. Grand Dad's features—slight frame, thinning grey hair, and amiable face marred slightly by a broken nose—remained unaltered after 20 years. He had never failed to indulge me by playing my childish games. He had always let me win. Grand Mom's beaming apple pie face, and the smell of her pastry flour cologne filled me with equally wonderful childhood memories. I was drawn back at a thirty degree angle toward the road where Ric had parked. The snow fell heavily now, and the relentless wind crept under my hood. I shivered. I witnessed the starkness of this place through crystalline flakes encrusted on my eyelashes.

I walked about forty feet through the deepening snow, then stopped. I knelt and dug vigorously. I reached a brass plaque, and brushed the snow from its left corner. Inch by inch, as my glove removed the snow, the Virgin Mary's image was revealed to me. The letters EVELYN became visible directly below the Virgin's image. My next stroke uncovered my grandmother's entire name, EVELYN M. O'CONNELL. I smiled, recalling her immense capacity to love and her devotion to the mother of Christ. I had inherited her fondness for animals, but not her religious devotion or her open heart. Thoughts of Grand Mom warmed me. I motioned for Ric to join me. Then I cleaned the rest of my grandmother's plaque.

By the time Ric got there, I had removed the snow from my grandfather's plaque, too. GEORGE EDWARD JOSEPH O'CONNELL. I looked up at Ric, and said, "I have found my grandparents."

Ric raised his brow and attempted a smile. The wreaths encircled both his arms. He reminded me of a circus juggler. Ric began securing the wreaths, and I moved several feet to the right. I dug into the snow and found the grave marker for Margaret W. Deering. She was not a relative; but as long as I could remember, no wreaths, or flowers were ever placed on her grave. That saddened me. So I decorated her's with a wreath, spring flowers, or whatever I placed on my relatives' graves. Margaret W. Deering will not be forgotten as long as I'm alive.

Ric's ears and cherubic cheeks were crimson, and his frosty eyelashes, beard, and moustache glistened. He tried to hide his discomfort. Ric did not complain. That was his way. I whispered my goodbyes. We returned to Ric's car in silence. Ric and I avoided eye contact as we brushed the snow from our jackets. Once inside, Ric started the engine. He gripped the steering wheel and stared out the window at the wipers whooshing away the newly-fallen layer of snow. While the engine warmed, Ric turned to me and said, "I don't want to know how you did that."

"Good." My glove over my mouth muffled my sigh of relief.

Suddenly, my thoughts returned to the present as a Geo Prism cut into my lane without signaling. I avoided it by easing off the accelerator. I had no idea how long I had been driving. A gargantuan tarp appeared to be covering the sky as I exited onto Route 50 toward Annapolis. Several minutes later, a curtain of rain approached from the southwest and pelted the interstate.

Just what I needed. I was unfamiliar with the area, and the heavy downpour made the road signs difficult to read. Being inept at directions and hating to drive under the best conditions, my resolve to find the missing police dog began to waver. I justified my increasing desire to give up and return home by convincing myself this rain would make it impossible for me to find our designated meeting place, Silesia Community Park. I would, therefore, be relieved of my commitment. I had not given Cmdr. Herschel my phone number so I . . . No. The police were running out of resources. I was certain their police dog was running out of time. I moved into the slow lane and kept driving.

Fifteen minutes later, I saw the exit I needed—Route 100-Gibson Island. I followed the remaining directions and arrived at two-fifteen p.m. Two police officers approached my station wagon as I pulled onto the parking lot.

I struggled to put on my slicker in those tight quarters while the shorter of the two officers motioned for me to roll down my window. I complied, turning the window handle spasmodically with my sleeve-covered left hand.

The officer said, "Miss St. George?" I nodded and continued fighting with the handle until the window was open completely. If I ever buy another car, it must have power windows.

"I'm Cmdr. Herschel and this is Sgt. Lawrence, our missing K-9's handler. We're sorry to make you come out in this weather. It's been pouring here all day. I was hoping by this time it would have stopped. We'll understand if you don't want to try to find our dog in this mess."

"No, officer," I said. " I feel very strongly we need to do this now. If we don't find him soon, it will be too late."

"All right then. If you think you can manage." Cmdr. Herschel and Sgt. Lawrence appeared undaunted by the weather. Their leathery faces and rough hands evidenced years of exposure to variable conditions. "Let's sit in our patrol car, and you tell us what you want to do."

En route to their car, I said, "First, I would like to sit in the back where your dog rides if you don't mind."

Sgt. Lawrence's wide-eyed stare amused me. He was a man's man—a hunter or fisherman. He at one time had been in top physical condition. Too many fast-food meals and too little exercise had, however, taken their toll. I surmised what Sgt. Lawrence was thinking about me. A strange woman called and offered to help the police search for their lost dog. Not that she had actually seen their dog. She had a vision of their dog in her mind. Right. This woman arrived in her Yuppie mobile looking like she stepped from the pages of *Town and Country*. She then wanted to climb into the dog compartment of our cruiser. Right.

Cmdr. Herschel's glare stopped Sgt. Lawrence before he could explain why I would not want to get into the dog's compartment. Realizing I was to be given anything I wanted no matter how ridiculous it sounded, Sgt. Lawrence ushered me into his cruiser.

I crawled around the compartment looking for something belonging to their dog. It smelled of dog, which was perfectly acceptable to me. I said, "During our conversation this morning, I forgot to ask you to bring something your dog touched—his collar or a toy. By the way, what's the dog's name?"

"Luke", Sgt. Lawrence called over his shoulder as he walked toward the back of his cruiser. He opened the trunk. "I usually keep several of Luke's balls and leads in here. Let me see. Here they are. Other dogs have touched these. Is that okay?"

As I looked up to answer, I noticed Cmdr. Herschel watching me through the driver's window. His puzzled stare and slack jaw gave me pause. He probably thought I was sniffing around trying to catch Luke's scent. I bolted up and noticed dog hair covered my knees and elbows. While I attempted to brush the hair from my chinos, I answered, "I believe so. I will be concentrating solely on Luke so hopefully I will see only him." Cmdr. Herschel opened the door and I crawled out. I smoothed some of the wrinkles from my pants then stood tall. I held my hand out. "Please give me Luke's things so I can give this a try."

Sgt. Lawrence handed me a ball and lead. I closed my eyes and focused on the objects in my hands. I envisioned a titian and black German Shepherd puppy playing with a five or six year old blonde girl. I related this scene to the officers, but Sgt. Lawrence assured me he was unmarried and had no children. I perceived a hint of pleasure as he insisted Luke was brown and black, not titian and black. Sgt. Lawrence's tone made it obvious he believed I was wasting his time.

I worried that the dog I had envisioned was not their missing K-9. I was about to confess my apprehension when Cmdr. Herschel remarked, "Hadn't we purchased Luke from a Hungarian breeder? And didn't someone mention that breeder had children?"

Sgt. Lawrence gazed into space apparently trying to jog his memory. "You know, Tom, now that you mention it, I do remember hearing Luke's breeder had children—several daughters, I think."

My confidence was renewed. I was on the right track. My mind shifted suddenly to my original vision of the dog in the woods. I turned quickly to Sgt. Lawrence and asked, "Can you show me exactly where you were when Luke got away from you?"

"Sure." I held Luke's belongings close to my heart as I followed Sgt. Lawrence to the edge of the park. Drizzle on my glasses caused rippled images like I was looking at the world through an old window. Sgt. Lawrence pointed toward a field on an adjacent farm as I wiped my glasses with my handkerchief. I walked in that direction. The officers followed. Sgt. Lawrence said that on the night Luke had run away, he remembered walking him through that field as usual. He thought the time was approximately eleven twenty-five p.m. because his shift ended at eleven p.m., and he walked Luke immediately after work. I recalled thinking Sgt. Lawrence inordinately concerned with the exact time of the incident, but I decided police training must have instilled in him the importance of pinpointing time.

Sgt. Lawrence said both he and Luke had been surprised by a rabbit that bolted from some underbrush. Luke had lunged at the rabbit and broken his raveled lead. He zigzagged across the field and headed toward the farmhouse. Sgt. Lawrence had pursued him, but had lost Luke in the darkness. I thought Sgt. Lawrence careless for using the unsafe lead, but decided to table the lecture as we approached the farmhouse.

Cmdr. Herschel described their department's search of the area; however, I tuned him out. I was certain Luke was not on the farm. I felt compelled to face west. My attention was inexplicably drawn toward a wooded area off in the distance, and I pointed in that direction. "I'm going to those woods."

I did not wait for their responses. I ran back across the field and parking lot toward the woods. Puddles and mud created a natural obstacle course. In my haste, I failed to notice the steep slope on the other side of the parking lot. That became strikingly apparent, however, the second my foot left the blacktop and connected with the wet grass. I slipped and fell backward. My right hand took the brunt as I slid down the misty hill like an apprentice acrobat. Pain pierced my hand and shot up through my arm and neck, but my left hand still clutched Luke's ball and lead. A wave of nausea enveloped me by the time I reached the bottom of the hill. I crouched for a minute and took several deep breaths. The nausea passed quickly so I continued running toward the woods.

When I reached the trees and my adrenalin rush ebbed, I realized the intensity of my pain. My long, slender fingers had already begun to swell. I shook my injured hand hoping the movement would help my circulation. Mud flew from my fingertips like grass from a Weedeater. I turned my face to the heavens and closed my eyes as I tracked in a tiny circle. I did not want those officers to see me like this. The cool rain felt restorative.

Only a miracle could have helped my appearance. The front of my chinos and slicker were spattered with mud. My hood had blown off. Long tendrils of my drenched hair stuck to my cheeks and dripped down the front of my slicker. As Cmdr. Herschel approached, I pulled my hood over my head then quickly hid my injured hand in my coat pocket. I was unwilling to bear witness to my foolhardiness.

Cmdr. Herschel's agility was impressive by comparison. If he was not a runner, then he certainly kept himself in excellent shape for a man, I would guess, in his late fifties. Cmdr. Herschel demanded with all the tact he could muster, "Miss St. George, you must stay with us! Running off by yourself in an unfamiliar area, you could have been hurt. Remember, you are a civilian, and it is our duty to protect you." I began to protest, but he continued firmly. "That is our rule. And, let me assure you, we will be by your side for the duration of our search."

As Cmdr. Herschel delivered his edict, I saw something lumbering toward us like a circus bear in a police costume. "What the hell . . . oh, excuse me." Sgt. Lawrence panted, bending over at the waist to catch his breath.

Cmdr. Herschel repeated slowly, "I was just telling Miss St. George that she must stay with us." He turned and looked me square in the eye. "Isn't that right Miss St. George?"

We stared at one another indignantly. I broke eye contact and took a step toward the woods. Cmdr. Herschel moved to my right and Sgt. Lawrence to my left. We resembled the Royal Lippizaners performing their famous pas de deux. Except ours was an awkward pas de trois.

I looked from one officer to the other then peered into the woods. Its murkiness was gothic. A chill slithered along my spine. On second thought, perhaps the officers' presence was comforting. We moved silently, shoulder-to-shoulder, along the perimeter of the woods. First to the right, then to the left . . . then to the right again. I sensed the officers were questioning my maneuvers, but I could offer no rational explanation. I only knew I needed to walk along those woods. They were the unwilling participants in my chorus line.

I thought I heard an animal sound emanating from the woods. I stopped abruptly. The two officers and I bumped into one another like members of the Keystone Cops. Sgt. Lawrence began to speak, but I held up my hand to silence him. I craned my neck toward the woods in an effort to discern the sound. I hoped my eagerness to find Luke had not caused me to imagine that I had heard something.

A twig snapped. I whirled right. Cmdr. Herschel's embarrassed grin and his shift back to his original position convinced me he was the origin of the sound. My expression registered my displeasure.

I turned my back to the woods and walked toward the parking lot. I was considering repeating the entire process when I heard the sound again. I paused and cocked my head toward the sound. Silence. The three of us became the trees. Silence. I spun on my heels anxiously, then trotted several feet inside the woods. I stopped abruptly again. This time, my body guards kept their distance. I was certain I recognized that sound. I looked from Cmdr. Herschel to Sgt. Lawrence and asked, "Do you hear that dog panting in the woods?"

Sgt. Lawrence rolled his eyes as if questioning whether I was from this planet. "No, Ma'am." He was unable to hide his amusement as he answered me.

"I hear a dog panting over there," I insisted, pointing fifteen degrees to my right. "I'm telling you, I can hear him."

Cmdr. Herschel's irritation was obvious. "I'm telling you, Miss St. George, our department has been scouring these woods for the last three days. We've used infrared helicopters, search dogs, and officers on foot and horseback. Our dog is not here."

In an obdurate tone I continued, "If Luke is not in these woods, then he is in another woods in that direction." I arched my arm to indicate I meant beyond the woods directly in front of us.

Cmdr. Herschel removed his cap and ran his fingers through his light hair, and replied, "There is a state park in that direction, but I don't think Luke could have gone that far."

"You're wrong. I have seen documented cases where animals have been found fifty, one hundred, five hundred miles from where they were lost. Please, Cmdr. Herschel, time is running out. Just take me to that park."

"Okay, it's your show," replied Cmdr. Herschel, as we rushed for their cruiser.

Sgt. Lawrence drove for what seemed like an eternity. The purring engine and the drone of the dispatcher's voice on the radio broke our silence. I sensed Luke was not in that park as we approached the ranger's station. But desperation prompted me to jump out of the cruiser as soon as we stopped and head into the forest. The two officers scrambled after me.

I jogged twenty to thirty feet along a path and stopped. I was certain Luke was not there. I turned to face Cmdr. Herschel, and shook my head. "This is a waste of precious time." I turned around and pointed my left hand. "I feel Luke is in *that* direction."

Cmdr. Herschel experienced an epiphany. "Miss St. George is pointing toward Silesia Community Park. Dave, she doesn't know this area. She must sense that Luke is back there. Let's go!"

We arrived at our destination in record time. I suspected our speedy return stemmed more from Sgt. Lawrence's impatience with the situation than his faith in me.

Fog had enveloped the park. "Let's approach the woods from the other side," I suggested. "Perhaps I will feel something different."

Our unlikely trio trooped along the hilltop then stood overlooking what looked to be the opposite side of the woods. If we did not find Luke soon, the decreasing visibility would end our search. Luke's lead and ball were enfolded in my arms as I held them close to my heart. My right hand still throbbed, but I didn't care. I closed my eyes, and stood perfectly still. I breathed deeply . . . slowly. I envisioned a titian and black German Shepherd sitting quietly on a stream's bank. Trees surrounded his resting place. His lead was caught on a branch of a downed tree. This scene matched the scene I saw this morning. I was sure this was the place.

I tried to control my excitement. "Walk down this hill and into the woods. Find the stream and follow it to the left. Near the woods' edge, you will find Luke. I'm certain of it!"

We carefully traversed the hill and entered the woods. Anticipation hung in the mist. Sgt. Lawrence and Cmdr. Herschel shot each other a sideward glance when we came upon a stream. Silently, Sgt. Lawrence explored the right bank and Cmdr. Herschel the left. The dense vegetation coupled with the fog hindered their search. I trailed behind the Commander. I was anxious yet afraid of what they would find.

The stillness in the woods was unnerving. I decided to call the dog's name. I thought that might prompt Luke to bark, and that would enable us to pinpoint his location. Plus, I would have something to do other than worry. "Luke. Luke, boy." I called repeatedly. Cmdr. Herschel and Sgt. Lawrence joined me.

After a quarter hour, we had found nothing. A sinking feeling came over me. I lagged farther and farther behind.

Self-doubt loomed above me in the branches overhead like tree snakes in a bayou. What a fool I had been. I was about to launch into my self-chastisement routine when I suddenly heard someone yell, "Oh my God!"

I held my breath and dug my heels into the mud. I was afraid to move. I could see a lone figure walking toward me. It was Cmdr. Herschel. "I'm terribly sorry to have wasted your time," I said. The Commander's response was interrupted by the trampling of underbrush on the opposite bank. I thought I saw a large, dark figure emerging from the mist. That figure then divided in two. I realized it was Sgt. Lawrence with his titian and black German Shepherd, Luke, by his side.

Chapter 2

Two days had passed since I had helped the Lennoxville Police Department find their dog, Luke. I was delighted by the dozen long-stemmed red roses the K-9 Division sent to my home.

Cmdr. Herschel had offered to pay me for helping them, but I had refused. After Sgt. Lawrence found Luke, they crossed the stream to join Cmdr. Herschel and me. Luke pulled the Sergeant directly toward me. Luke's tail wagged exuberantly as he danced at my feet. I knelt and hugged his neck. To the astonishment of Sgt. Lawrence, Luke planted a canine kiss from my chin to my forehead. That kiss was reward enough for me. I realized at that moment that if I had accomplished nothing else in my lifetime, helping to save Luke would have been enough.

Luke appeared hungry and dehydrated, so I insisted that he be taken to a vet for a checkup immediately. Sgt. Lawrence promised he would, then called that evening to report my assessment had been correct. He said that Luke would be fine after a course of subcutaneous fluids and several hearty meals.

Cmdr. Herschel, despite my objections, had credited me with Luke's rescue and labeled me a psychic. He had advised me the media would insist on a story. We agreed he could furnish them with all of the details except one—my name. I was certain my partners in the firm would be less than enthusiastic if they learned of my contribution to Luke's rescue. A large, old-line accounting firm could do without that type of publicity.

The media had a field day with the story. Local channels filmed their reporters attempting to recreate Luke's rescue. Reporters crawled around the dog compartment of Sgt. Lawrence's cruiser, clutching Luke's ball and lead while staring skyward. They waded through ankle-deep mud re-enacting our search. They, however, lacked the foresight to wear Wellingtons.

Monday, the newspapers in both Baltimore and Washington ran front-page articles, "Psychic Locates Lost Police Dog in Woods," and "Lennoxville Police Use Psychic to Collar Missing Canine". Cmdr. Herschel left a message on my answering machine advising he was being barraged with requests for information about the psychic. The calls ranged from CNN to the National Enquirer to The Oprah Winfrey Show. He teased that had he accepted the bribes offered to identify the psychic, he could have been set for life. He was compiling a list of callers and their requests in case I might want to contact them at some later date. I did not want to appear ungrateful; I refrained from mentioning my plan to file his list in my circular file.

Each time I spoke to my mother since the story had broken, she prattled on about "the unique gifts of that talented psychic. His or her mother should be very proud." However, I knew from past experience any other talented psychic's mother would have been proud. Not mine. How would she explain her daughter's aberrant behavior to the members of her bridge and garden clubs?

Coverage of Luke's rescue prompted kudos for the psychic from the animal lovers in the office and skepticism from the others. I feigned ignorance of the entire story. No one thought that strange because they knew I was preparing for a horse show and had little time to read the newspaper. Everyone also knew I preferred books to television.

I confessed my part in Luke's rescue to my closest friends and swore them to secrecy. To my amazement, none were shocked. Each related long-forgotten incidents where I had exhibited psychic abilities but had shrugged them off as coincidental. Always business-minded, all except Ric urged me to go public and capitalize on the notoriety. I declined, hoping a new story would soon catch the media's attention.

Wednesday evening I returned from horseback riding around 8:30 p.m. All I could think about as I pulled into my driveway was the relief I would feel after removing my uncomfortable bra. I always resented having to wear that thing. When bra burning was popular on college campuses, I actually considered igniting a few of mine . . . especially the underwires. It has never been proven, but I suspect brassieres were the torturous invention of a crazed misogynist.

I balanced my business uniform, briefcase, and riding crop as I unlocked the back door. The telephone in my kitchen began to ring as I depressed the wrought iron door latch and opened the door. I hoped it was not an emergency at the office. Whenever I ride instead of working late, a crisis invariably arises.

The dogs pushed past me and ran out into the garden. I dropped everything except my suit onto the kitchen table, and grabbed the wall phone's receiver before the answering machine clicked on. A gravelly voice on the other end said, "Ms. St. George, this is Harry Templeton from *The Sun*. I need to talk to you about the police dog."

I was speechless. My hands froze around both the receiver and the suit hanger. I stared into the receiver as if I might be able to see the intruder. I realized my secret was out.

"Ms. St. George," the voice began again, "are you there?"

"You have the wrong number," I replied and slammed the receiver into its cradle defiantly. That should be the end of that.

I was startled when the phone rang again before I could remove my hand. I backed away quickly, and toppled over a chair. My crisp linen suit slid across the tile floor and came to rest in a wrinkled heap against the dishwasher. My clumsiness scattered my feline companions who had gathered to greet me.

I got up and rushed to my desk in the library where the answering machine would screen the call.

"Ms. St. George, this is Harry Templeton from *The Sun*, again. Damn I hate these machines. I know this is your number. I got it from the phone company. I know you're there. Come on. Pick up."

What is wrong with those people at the telephone company giving out my number without my permission? They will certainly hear about this. Wait a minute, I have a listed number. They do have my permission. Of course they gave my number out.

I eased into my cordovan leather desk chair and breathed deeply. I must not allow this pesky person to unnerve me. I inhaled and exhaled several times. If I simply refuse to answer, he will give up.

Believing my tenacity was surpassed only by my cats', I returned to the kitchen to retrieve my suit before one of my feline mafia danced the kitty cha cha on it.

Too late. Guinevere, Ariel, and Percival already samba'd on my suit to protest my failure to feed them immediately upon entering the house. I doubted linen and cat fur would be a popular blend this season. The rest of the motley crew glowered as I scurried around the kitchen preparing their dinner.

I wondered as I counted out steel cat dishes how Harry Templeton got my name. The police assured me my identity would be kept confidential. The media will hound me if my name had leaked out. I can imagine the headlines, "Psychic CPA Finds Police Dog". People will queue outside my door demanding lotto numbers. What will this do to my standing in the community? What will my partners think?

I was opening a can of cat food when the phone rang again. The automatic can opener made several passes around the can before I disengaged the pressure. I allowed the answering machine to screen my call. I heard kitty paws follow as I ran to the library to listen to the message. My companion animals were unaccustomed to having their dinner preparation interrupted.

His coarse voice was becoming familiar. "Ms. St. George why don't you pick up the damned phone? Look, I just want to talk to you." The voice paused, "I'm going to talk to you one way or another, so what's it going to be . . . at your home or at your office?"

This man surely would not have the audacity to bother me at my office. I chewed the inside of my lip. Then I smiled. He can't disturb me at the office. I will ensure he won't get past our security guards. First thing tomorrow, I will insist Harry Templeton be refused admittance to the building. I grinned with self-satisfaction. I will also inform my secretary, Suzy, I do not wish to speak to Mr. Templeton for any reason. I felt securely in control again. I took several deep breaths then returned to the kitchen to feed the angry mob.

*   *   *

Thursday my business day was filled with meetings, personnel crises, and more meetings. At five p.m., I was finally able to sit at my desk and work on my projects. I worked another four hours until the numbers became a blur. I drove home where the evening ritual began. I fed the crew, played fetch with the dogs, then prepared a spinach salad for dinner.

I sat at the kitchen table eating my salad and rereading Thomas Hardy's *Jude the Obscure*, my favorite novel. I shun contemporary authors and prefer the Victorians and Pre-Raphaelites. I contend the world prior to 1920 was more civilized despite all the miracles of modern technology and medicine. My friend Ric, a professor of contemporary literature at Johns Hopkins University, often teased that one day he would drag me kicking and screaming into the twenty-first century.

I savored a shallot and read, "—when our minds were clear, and our love of truth fearless—the time was not ripe for us! Our ideas were fifty years too soon to be any good to us." Recently, I found myself longing to feel the passion for someone that Sue felt for Jude.

The ring of the phone interrupted my musing. I reached for the wall phone, then withdrew my hand as from a hot stove. In case it was Harry Templeton, I decided to let the answering machine answer. I hurried to the library to listen to the message.

The caller said, "Katherine."

I snatched the receiver when I recognized Ric's voice. I perched on the side of the massive walnut counting house table I used as my desk.

"Hi. I am so glad it's you. I was afraid you were that reporter."

"Katherine, would you just forget about Harry Templeton." Ric's tone warned my paranoia was getting old. "You sounded upset when you told me about him this morning and now you are mentioning him again. Let it go. He's probably after some other quarry by now."

"You're right. I'm taking this too seriously. Have you found a substitute for our match on Sunday?"

"No, that's partially why I called. I have several possibilities, and each is reported to be an excellent tennis player. But since that comes from members of the engineering faculty, I plan to check them out then make my selection." Ric paused and cleared his throat. "I know you are not going to appreciate this, Katherine, but the club switched our court time to Saturday at noon in order to accommodate a large party."

"Saturday I planned to practice for my horse show."

"I know. But surely you can practice on Sunday instead." I could hear a piece of fabric rubbing against the receiver; Ric was probably putting on a blazer. "I must go. My date's pulling into the driveway. I'll see you Saturday. Bye."

His date had arrived. I moved to my desk chair and snuggled in. I wondered why men don't pick up their dates anymore. Perhaps I'm old fashioned or perhaps I just hate to drive, but I like being chauffeured around. I thought that was a man's job.

The phone rang again. Must not have been Ric's date. I leaned back in my chair and lifted the receiver slowly. I intended to have fun with Ric. "Have such a harem you don't recognize all of their cars?"

Instead of Ric's parry there was a brief silence. Then the unwelcome voice said, "Ms. St. George, this is Harry Templeton from *The Sun*."

I snapped to attention and replied with what Colin had called surgical precision, "I have nothing to say to you." I hung up and looked heavenward. Please make Harry Templeton go away!

*   *   *

Many Baltimoreans seek relief from the heat and humidity by weekending either in the mountains or at the ocean. Both are equidistant from Charm City. My secretary, Suzy, was a sun worshiper and stubbornly ignored my warnings about the hazards of overexposure to the sun. I think she was under the mistaken assumption a dark tan would accentuate her dyed blonde hair and miraculously camouflage her extra fifty pounds. Her parents owned a condo at Ocean City which she used practically every weekend. I knew Suzy disliked the weekend beach traffic; therefore, I routinely suggested she take a half day off on Fridays and leave for the beach early.

This particular Friday afternoon was busy but nothing I could not handle myself. I had no meetings scheduled, and all of my projects were progressing smoothly. The humidity was lower than it had been in weeks, so I decided to leave early myself and go riding.

As I sat at Suzy's L-shaped desk in our reception room switching our telephones to voice mail, a disheveled man entered. His clothes were quality but outdated, and he appeared hesitant to speak. He reeked of stale cigars—even from across the room—and the grease spot on his club tie was the size of a silver dollar. With his ruddy complexion and wide girth, the only things missing were a beard, red flannel suit, and reindeer. His white hair was thinning and rested on his shirt collar, and he appeared to be in his sixties. He was the antithesis of our usual clients.

"May I help you?" I smiled at the thought of my early departure, not his arrival.

"Yes, I have an appointment with Ms. St. George," the man replied tentatively, peeking over his black wire-rimmed half glasses and brushing a wisp of hair off his forehead.

His voice sounded like sand paper rubbing against wood. Had I forgotten this appointment? I was certain my calendar was free for the remainder of the afternoon. He approached the desk as I scoured Suzy's desk calendar.

"Don't be embarrassed. Ms. St. George and I made the appointment just this morning. She probably forgot to mention it. He added jovially, "You know how bosses are."

I was about to identify myself, when I realized his voice was all too familiar. I sprang up, shoving Suzy's chair backward with such force it slammed against the wall between our offices. I leaned on both hands and glared at him across the desk. He stepped around the right side of the desk and started toward me.

"Harry Templeton!" I snapped, feeling my face flush with anger and my jaw tighten. "How did you get in here? I left instructions with the guards that YOU were not allowed in this building." I picked up the receiver. "I'm calling security. They'll escort you out."

As I dialed, he lunged toward me and snatched the receiver from my hand. "Now listen to me Ms. St. George," he growled as he shook the receiver at my face. "I tried calling you several times, and you refused to talk to me. I must talk to you, and you left me no choice."

I backed away as if he were a leper. I stepped to the other side, keeping the desk between us. I kept my eyes peeled on him as I backed toward the door.

"We'll see what choices you have when security arrives," I retorted as I fumbled for the door knob behind me. I flung open the door and fled down the hall.

Harry hung on the doorframe and called after me, "When they get here, I'll be forced to tell them I've come to interview you about Luke."

I stopped midstep, hoping no one had heard him. I retreated quickly to Suzy's office and closed the door behind me. I decided reluctantly to placate him.

Men generally find me attractive for some reason which escapes me. I have used that to my advantage on occasion, but only in a decorous way. This was definitely one of those occasions.

"Harry. You don't mind me calling you Harry, do you?" I grinned begrudgingly. "Let's be reasonable about this. We would not want to do anything we'll regret." I remained stationed at the door, waiting to take my cue from Harry.

"More to the point, you hope I won't do anything you'll regret," Harry replied as he flopped into Suzy's chair. Harry plunked his feet on top of the desk obviously savoring his temporary control.

His scuffed black wingtips scattered Suzy's pens and papers across her desk. Suzy shared my penchant for neatness; I made a mental note to straighten her desk before leaving.

Harry locked his fingers behind his head and leaned back. "Katherine. You don't mind me calling you Katherine, do you?" Harry did not wait for my reply. "You know, you remind me of young Kate Hepburn despite your long blonde hair. You both have that patrician air about you."

Patrician. Ric often described me as patrician, but I thought he was joking. I supposed I should have been insulted, but I was not. I like Katherine Hepburn. I don't care what Harry Templeton thinks of me.

"Katherine . . . no . . . Kate. Yes, Kate suits you."

"Excuse me. I prefer to be called Katherine," I tossed over my shoulder as I walked across the office toward the window.

"Kate, unless you want all the media on the East Coast to know your name, you must hear me out. I've gone to a lot of trouble to find you."

I'll bet you have, I thought. I felt my jaw tightening again. I decided to be casual and pretend to be interested in something outside, "By the way, how did you manage to find me?"

"I told the security guards I was your uncle from Denver. I said I was in town on business and wanted to surprise you. They were so obliging, they escorted me directly to your office."

No Christmas bonuses for them. I will talk to the head of security first thing Monday morning.

I meandered around the office feigning nonchalance

but inconspicuously keeping my eye on Harry. I found his appearance distasteful. I was humiliated by the thought of anyone believing this sartorial nightmare was related to me. "No Harry, I meant how did you learn my name?"

"Got lucky, I guess," Harry answered proudly. "Tom Herschel and I go way back, you see. I went to talk to him late yesterday about a murder case I've been covering. I no sooner sat down than Tom started raving about the psychic who saved his dog, Luke. He just went on and on about how amazing this person was." Harry leisurely removed his feet from the desk, rested his elbows on the desk pad, and supported his double chin with his palms. "Hey Kate, I sure could use a cup of coffee. I'll bet there's coffee somewhere in this office. Would you make me a cup?"

The hair stood up on the back of my neck. I temporarily forgot my ploy. I whirled around, marched to the desk and stretched across it until our noses almost touched. The words shot out before I could catch myself. "Harry, this is not a social call. There is no coffee. And if there was, I would not give you a cup. So just cut to the chase." I immediately realized my faux pas and slowly removed myself from his space. I managed a fake smile as I retreated to one of the Queen Anne chairs in front of the bookcase. I hoped Harry was a bottom line kind of person.

"You're right, Kate. I should get to the point." Harry appeared undaunted by my attack. "I battered Tom with questions about his wonderful psychic. Man or woman? Young or old? Worked in D.C.? Lived in D.C.? Tom wouldn't budge. He said he promised to protect the psychic's privacy, and that was what he intended to do." Harry's tone reflected his remembered frustration.

My annoyance with his stale cigar cologne paled compared to my annoyance with Harry in general. I twirled my hair around my index finger impatiently as I repeated, "So how did you learn my name?"

"Used a trick of the trade." Harry doodled on Suzy's notepad with his Montblanc pen. "Tom was called out of his office for an emergency. I snooped around while he was gone. I looked in the obvious hiding places, desk drawers and filing cabinet. Nothing. I sat at his desk to have a smoke and devise a new plan. My lighter was empty so I rummaged through some papers on his desk looking for a pack of matches. A tiny slip of paper caught my eye. And bingo!

Harry straightened himself in Suzy's chair. He stared into my eyes then pointed his pen at the ceiling. "I tell you, Kate, it was providence."

I held his stare. Both Harry's solemnity and choice of pens surprised me.

"I picked up the paper. There were a florist's name and address, and yours." Harry shook his head. "If it had been any other man, I would have thought he was having an affair. Not Tom. He is a real straight arrow. So I surmised you were the psychic, and he sent you flowers to thank you for finding his dog."

My anger flared. I wondered how Cmdr. Herschel could have been so careless. He promised to protect me. Men. I tried to maintain my facade. "Does Cmdr. Herschel know you found my name?"

"Hell no. Do you really think I would be stupid enough to tell him? Don't answer that," Harry chuckled. Harry Templeton was not a man who took himself too seriously.

My answer would have been witty but caustic; I refrained. God forbid, I should alienate him.

Harry continued, "I left Tom a note offering some lame excuse for leaving. Then I went to a restaurant to call you."

I had to know, "Why didn't you call from your cell phone?"

"Don't have one. Don't believe in them," Harry defended himself. "I'm uncomfortable with all this new technology. You need a damn doctorate in computer science to use all that stuff. Hell, I still write my copy on a typewriter. My editor bought me an electric one for Christmas last year, and I have no trouble using it." Harry puffed with pride.

Harry Templeton was a dinosaur. I use state-of-the-art computer systems; Harry probably cannot find the ON/OFF switch. My self-proclaimed superiority felt good.

Harry rose, stretched, and wandered around, examining Suzy's art treasures. She had wanted to choose the artwork for her office so I had given her a budget and hoped she would use some tasteful creativity. By Suzy's own admission, her parents were nouveau riche Towsonites who contended appropriate home furnishings were limited to cherry Queen Anne reproductions from Pennsylvania House. Suzy inherited their decorating biases. Her office walls were adorned with botanical prints and hunt scenes even though she could not distinguish a peony from a foxglove, or an Andalusian from a Clydesdale. I once envisioned Suzy's massive buttocks astride an English saddle. It was not a graceful sight.

When Suzy showed me the artwork she had purchased, I remember being relieved that Suzy's taste in art was diametrically opposed to her taste in business attire. Suzy believed black had a slimming effect and wore it ninety percent of the time. Most of our staff joked that Suzy was in a state of perpetual mourning.

Harry ran his smoke-stained index finger along the carved frame of a Herring hunt scene. "I hadn't eaten all day, so I went into a sub shop, grabbed a sandwich, then called you. You know, I used all my quarters on that call." Harry turned to me and complained, "I got a parking ticket this morning because I had no quarters for the meter. So, you owe me, Kate." Harry laughed heartily.

I chuckled momentarily, then postured. "You have not explained why you wanted to speak to me."

Harry looked at me soberly, "Is there someplace we could talk privately?"

"We can talk right here. This is private enough."

"Look, Kate, this is your place of business. What I want to talk to you about has nothing to do with business. Its personal. And this office with its mahogany paneling and damask drapes is stuffy. I'm surprised that philodendron survives in this room. I feel like I'm in my lawyer's office." Harry shifted his weight and rolled his neck and shoulders in discomfort.

Colin's law office was decorated much the same as mine. I saw nothing wrong with our taste. Harry obviously disliked formality. Or, he had been the defendant in too many lawsuits. Probably a combination of both.

I am a skeptic so I balked at his proposal. I thought aloud. "I wonder whether I should."

"Come on, Kate. Look at me. Do I look like a guy who plans to put the moves on you or any woman for that matter?" His Santa Claus face looked sincere. "Besides, as tall and slender as you are, you could outrun these stumpy legs even if you were wearing spiked heels." Harry added as an afterthought, "Which, of course, you're not. You seem too sensible to wear those things."

I felt foolish and my expression betrayed me. "As you wish, Harry. We can walk to the Mt. Washington Tavern from here. We'll have a drink and talk."

So much for my horse show practice. I wished Harry Templeton would go away.

Chapter 3

When I suggested Harry and I go to the Mt. Washington Tavern, I had forgotten the corporate crowd met there on Fridays for Happy Hour. The place was crowded as usual.

The trend for many Baltimore-based businesses within the last decade has been to move their headquarters from downtown to the Mt. Washington, Towson, and Timonium corridor just north of the city. These relocations ostensibly were to relieve employees of downtown parking expenses and reduce Baltimore's traffic problems. In reality, those corporations wanted to escape the city's heavy corporate taxes. Mt. Washington, Towson, and Timonium now suffer from those very maladies which previously plagued Baltimore.

Mt. Washington's renaissance produced a plethora of restaurants and boutiques. The Mt. Washington Tavern is an upscale restaurant and bar in an abandoned warehouse.

It was six p.m. when my unwanted companion and I arrived. As we maneuvered past the suits and chinos with navy blazers lining the oak bar, I noticed Harry's reflection in the immense mirrored wall behind the liquor offerings. Was he really that old or had his life been that difficult?

Jerry, one of our security guards, was sitting at the far end of the u-shaped bar. Harry recognized Jerry and hurried past him. As I walked by Jerry whispered, "Ms. St. George, how'd you like your surprise?"

I was preoccupied with concealing Harry from any of my associates who might have lingered for another round. My blank look caused Jerry to stop munching beer nuts long enough to explain.

"You know . . . your uncle. He seemed real anxious to see you." Jerry beamed, indicating either a genuine interest in our reunion or too many Molsons.

I tapped Harry's fleeing shoulder and pointed him toward the back wall lined with booths. I craned my neck back toward Jerry while flashing my well-practiced smile and replied softly, "My uncle. Yes, he certainly *was* a surprise. Let's keep his visit between us." I hoped Jerry missed my up-curled lip.

Harry sat in the corner booth with his back to the wall. From his seat, he enjoyed a panoramic view. I grudgingly took a seat on the opposite bench with my back to the crowd. I wondered if Harry had taken the Hemingway seat to irritate me. I was being ridiculous. Harry could not have known that was my seat of choice. According to Feng Shui, the oriental art of placement, Harry had taken the command position. And that was exactly where I preferred to be.

I was still settling in when Harry stuck a cigar in his mouth and mumbled a few syllables that sounded like, "Mind if I smoke?"

"As a matter of fact, I do." I declared incredulously. Why Harry's actions shocked me after more than an hour with him, I have no idea. "In case you haven't heard or have conveniently forgotten, Maryland law prohibits smoking in public places. And, that includes restaurants and bars. So get rid of that thing."

I grabbed the vile weed before he could utter a protest, and threw it under the table, crushing it with my shoe. Harry's pebble grey eyes became boulders. Harry Templeton was speechless.

I perceived I had better soften the blow. I added quietly, "Harry, you know smoking is bad for your health. Do you want to die young?"

"I don't damn well care when I die," he huffed. "Besides, I'm too old to die young." Harry scrambled under the trestle table knocking the checked table linens askew while he attempted to retrieve his cigar. He groaned and sat upright, holding the squashed cigar between his right index finger and his thumb. Harry raised it above his head in tribute. "Now look what you've done." Harry pounded his fist on the table twice. The silverware clanged. Harry sniveled, "That was my last cigar."

Fortunately for me the bar was noisy. Fortunately for Harry his performance went unnoticed. Harry's misery was gratifying yet perplexing. I found addictions untenable.

"If you must, you can replenish your cigar supply when you leave here," I said half-heartedly. I allowed Harry to mourn his fallen friend for a minute or two before asking, "Tell me Harry, how do you expect me to help you with your personal problems?"

Harry glanced at me sheepishly. "This is not exactly a personal problem," Harry replied slowly. He glanced around the bar to avoid my stare. I wondered why Harry was stalling. "Let's order a drink." Harry obviously substituted one addiction for another. "Where's the waitress?"

"They wait tables only in the restaurant. You must place our drink order at the bar." I snapped impatiently.

Harry stood obediently. I answered before he could ask what I wanted. "Nonalcoholic iced tea, and don't forget napkins." I dismissed Harry with a wave of my right hand while drumming on the table with my left. I would be here all night at this rate.

While Harry was gone, I seized the opportunity to scan the room for people I knew or, more to the point, for people I would not want to see me with Harry.

I liked the tavern's decor. Interior and exterior walls were half glass, half oak barn siding. Antique brass light fixtures sporting vivid green globes cast a hazy glow reminiscent of the gaslight they once emanated. Luxuriant ferns in tan wicker baskets hung from the ceiling on gleaming brass chains. Early photographs depicting Mt. Washington as a mill town were displayed on the walls, an unintentional reminder of its humble origins. The green and white chair cushions matched the table linens. Everything appeared crisp and clean.

Harry slid back into the booth. I noticed an orangish stain on the front of his dingy white shirt. He probably ate a Slim Jim while waiting for our drinks. Harry handed me my iced tea with a paper napkin. He slowly peeled the layers of napkin away from his drink, and caressed his glass as a lover would disrobe then fondle his beloved.

It was none of my business, but I wanted affirmation that my instincts were correct. "Rum and Coke?" I inquired as I poured a packet of unrefined sugar into my tea.

"Just Coke," Harry sighed. "I don't drink alcohol anymore."

I did not want to know any more about Harry Templeton than was absolutely necessary so I changed the subject. "Harry, what is this 'not exactly a personal problem' you believe I can help you with?"

"Guess I'd better start at the beginning."

I felt I would soon regret it, but I answered, "Please do."

Harry propped himself against the corner of the booth and loosened his tie. "About two-and-a-half weeks ago, my college roommate, Roy Allnutt, and I were to attend our thirty-year reunion at Boston College. I called Roy three days before we were scheduled to leave to discuss details and get directions. I had visited his place many years ago, but you know how you forget things over time." Harry paused and removed his Montblanc pen from his breast pocket. He began doodling on his paper napkin. "The response to my call was very strange."

I wanted to keep his monologue flowing so I asked, "Strange in what way, Harry?"

"Well, his daughter, Rowena, answered and sounded surprised when I asked for Roy. I explained we had planned to drive to the reunion together. Rowena interrupted and insisted I was mistaken. She said Roy had left several days before. To be honest, she mentioned the date, but I've forgotten exactly what she said."

I detected no problem. A man who could not remember to press his suit and polish his shoes would surely be a man who could not remember dates.

"I don't think that's strange." I accused Harry before I could rein in my tongue. "You probably had your dates confused. Or, perhaps you and your friend, what's his name again?"

"Roy . . . Roy Allnutt."

"Yes, your friend, Roy, could have agreed to depart on the date his daughter mentioned. I feel certain Roy remembers your habits. And when you failed to arrive on that date, Roy assumed you were busy with a story and forgot to call to advise him you could not come. So, he departed alone."

Harry considered that possibility.

I allowed Harry the benefit of the doubt and added, "Perhaps Roy had the dates confused."

"No, absolutely not." Harry bristled indignantly as he reached across the table and pointed his Montblanc at my nose. The tips almost collided.

My steadfast stare disarmed him. He retracted his weapon. "You're right about one thing, Kate." Harry's repentant eyes joined mine. "I'm a notorious 'no show'. Or, at least, I was until I stopped drinking."

And when was that—last week? To my dismay, I wanted to believe Harry. I wondered why I am the person everyone comes to when they have problems. Katherine is a good listener. She will help fix me. But, who will help fix me? No. Not this time. I broke our gaze. I squirmed and rubbed the right side of my neck. I wished Harry would get on with his story.

"Roy never confused dates. He majored in Business and was a whiz with numbers." Harry took a swig of Coke, then commenced doodling.

I reminded Harry, "Just because Roy was good with numbers, doesn't mean he could remember dates."

"Yes he could." Harry peered at me over his half glasses. "Roy was such a stickler for punctuality, he carried his date book everywhere."

Harry gulped his Coke. Then he threw back his head and laughed uproariously, "Well hell, he had to! Roy Allnutt had so many damn, oh excuse me, Kate, so many women running after him, he needed a date book to stay out of trouble. You know, picking up the wrong girl on the wrong day." Harry tried to contain himself. "I tell you, in those days, Roy had quite a life. He never studied, and got A's. But his parents wouldn't have cared if he failed. They just kept paying his bills and allowing him to do whatever he wanted. Roy could do no wrong according to them. They never said 'no' to Roy. He was their eldest son and heir to the estate." Harry scratched his head thoughtfully and sighed, "I envied his lifestyle while I had to slave over the books. I was in college on a full scholarship, and I had to maintain my grades." Harry took one last swallow and wiped his mouth with his napkin. Blue ink smudged his lips and chin as too many wild blueberries discolor a greedy child's face.

I shuddered. "Harry, watch what you're doing. You rubbed ink on your face," I scolded. "Go and wash it off." I shook my head and looked heavenward for assistance. I massaged my fingers against my temples and whispered, "Please don't let anyone I know see me with this buffoon."

Harry examined his napkin in disbelief. "Kate, don't be

so persnickety." Harry snatched my paper napkin and made a futile attempt to remove his ink splotches. "I'll bet you've worked hard all day yet you sit there in your pristine linen suit and your immaculate white blouse," Harry grumbled. "Not one of your hairs is out of place. I'll bet most women would like to know your secret." Harry studied me while scratching his five o'clock shadow. "Maybe it's the hair band." Harry tapped the side of his head where a hair band would have been. "Roy was always neat. In fact, he was constantly on me because I wasn't. You know, you two would have made the perfect couple."

Harry's opinion was inconsequential. However, if Harry thought his friend was too neat then Roy must have had some redeeming qualities. I wondered how those two had been roommates and remained friends over the years. I knew better than to ask if I wanted to get home at some point.

Harry threw my napkin down on the table and stood up. "You win, Kate. I need another drink anyway, so I might as well make you happy while I'm up."

I grinned like a Cheshire cat. The only way Harry Templeton could make me happy was to go away.

While I pondered that appealing eventuality, someone approached from my left and touched my shoulder. The weight of the hand suggested it belonged to a man. I instinctively flung the hand off my shoulder. My jaw tightened as I turned to face the presumptuous person.

Ric bent forward and kissed my forehead. "You look smug. What is that bean-counter brain of yours planning?"

My jaw relaxed as I answered, "What a pleasant surprise. Me? I'm not planning anything."

"Come now, Katherine." Ric's lapis eyes played beneath his tortoise shell glasses. "You are always planning something, even if it's merely the quickest route home."

"Guilty as charged. Let me guess why you're here."

Devilment overcame me, "No, no don't tell me." My raised hands halted Ric's answer. "You're meeting a date."

"You think you're so clever. However, tonight you're wrong." Ric sipped my iced tea, then grimaced when he tasted no alcohol. "I had a late meeting with the department chair, so I stopped on my way home to have a sandwich."

I do not like anyone standing over me so I motioned for Ric to sit in Harry's seat. I hoped that when Harry returned, he would get the hint and leave.

Ric slid across the bench and settled in. He asked, "More to the point, Katherine, why are you here? Aren't you supposed to be practicing for the horse show at Havenwood? You're so persnickety, you usually train and groom Flute daily the last two weeks before a show."

"Excuse me. That is the second time today I have been called persnickety. Not that I am being defensive, but let me tell you something, Mr. Rodric Henderson Whitby, III. I do not appreciate you or anyone else, for that matter . . ."

"Could I get a little help here?" Harry wavered at our table's edge. He precariously balanced a crowded round tray in his right hand, and a pizza tray in his left. Ric rose immediately and took the pizza tray from Harry. That knocked Harry off balance. He heeled over propelling a glass iced tea pitcher on the other tray directly at me. I thrust myself across the bench, as the pitcher glanced off the corner of the table and crashed to the floor.

Waiters ran from every direction. Our table was suddenly in the spotlight. Ric and Harry appeared amused as I supervised the clean up.

Fifteen minutes later, we three sat silently in our booth. Ric and Harry on the Hemingway side, me with my back to the gaping crowd. So much for maintaining a low profile.

Harry reached over and shook Ric's hand, "Harry Templeton, it's a pleasure to meet you." Harry gave each of us a slice of cold pizza.

"Harry Templeton?" Ric looked from Harry to me then back to Harry. He accepted the pizza and looked at me quizzically. I knew Ric would expect an explanation later. Ric poured himself a glass of Coke and smiled tentatively. "*The Sun*'s crime beat?"

"Right you are, my boy." Harry's face intimated his public recognition was in short supply. "Years ago, I worked the crime beat for the *New York Times*." Regret filled Harry's voice as he lowered his eyes. "But things happen, and fortune's change. That's life." Harry's voice trailed off. His chin sank to his chest and rested there. Harry looked like a wounded soldier who had taken his final breath.

I excused myself and retreated to the ladies room. I soaked a paper towel in cool water. I dabbed my face with the soothing towel, and confronted the all too familiar woman in the mirror. Harry Templeton was in pain. I was torn. I wanted to know the cause, but I didn't want to be responsible for helping him cope with it.

I rested my palms on the marble vanity and leaned closer to the image of the person I showed the world. I studied her angular face, her intense violet eyes. Why am I sympathizing with Harry? I asked myself. He is nothing to me but a thorn in my side. He is a loose canon and could sabotage everything I have worked for. I must simply placate him and then, hopefully, he will go away.

I freshened my lipstick, then removed my thin tortoiseshell hair band. Harry's disheartened face invaded my thoughts as I brushed my hair. I found it difficult to convince myself Harry was undeserving of my concern.

I returned to our booth to find Harry and Ric seemingly enjoying each other's company. I cut the slice of cold pizza on my plate.

Harry teased, "Kate, do you always eat pizza with a knife and fork?"

Ric chimed in before I could answer, "Yes. She can't stand

anything messy on her hands." He ignored my look of warning and continued jovially, "In fact, Harry, she cannot tolerate being dirty. Even when horseback riding, Katherine never gets mussed. I have seen her fall taking a fence," Ric raised his right hand. "And when she gets up, I swear, she looks as clean as she did before hitting the ground."

I put my utensils down and pushed the plate away. I could feel my jaw tightening as I aimed my barb at Harry. "I see nothing wrong with cleanliness." I took a calming breath and sipped my watery iced tea. "Harry, let's return to your friend, Roy Allnutt. What has he got to do with me?"

Harry shoved his last piece of pizza crust into his mouth then wiped his lips. "As I told you before Ric joined us, Roy's daughter's story just did not sit right with me. Roy would not have left for the reunion without calling me first."

Harry reached for my discarded pizza and placed it on his plate.

My disapproving glance prompted Harry to add, "I hate to waste food." Harry took a bite of my pizza. "Anyway, when I got to the reunion, I couldn't find Roy. I asked anyone and everyone if they had seen him. The answer was always the same—no. I tell you it was creepy. Roy seemed to have disappeared."

"I agree the circumstances seem strange." I was reluctant to ask, "but what has that got to do with me?"

Ric surmised Harry's reply and offered exuberantly, "Harry wants you to use your psychic abilities to find Roy!"

"Precisely," Harry affirmed.

"No. Finding Luke was a once in a lifetime fluke, and I refuse to try again." I clenched my clammy fists as I turned to Harry. "And you can't make me."

Harry's sly grin gave me pause. "You are absolutely right, Kate. I can't make you. However, if you don't help me, I'll tell the media about you and Luke."

"That's blackmail!" I screeched as I looked to Ric for support.

Ric offered none but answered instead, "Not exactly, Katherine. Harry's not asking for your money, only your help." Ric reached across the table and touched my hand. "Besides, what would it hurt? You've always been great at finding things."

"But a person? I've never been asked to find a person." I hoped they would see the absurdity of Harry's request.

"If you can find a dog, you can find a person," Harry concluded. "And, if you refuse to help me, I swear your name will be on the front page of every newspaper on the East Coast."

Chapter 4

At nine forty-five the next morning I pulled into the parking lot at Ellicott City's Railroad Museum. Ellicott City was only a five-minute drive from my home, so I thought that was a convenient place to meet Harry Templeton.

Ellicott City's narrow, serpentine main street hugs the entrances to row houses once inhabited by mill workers. The promise of steady work had attracted men and their families to the booming mid-nineteenth century town carved into jagged stone outcroppings along the Patapsco River. The main street was a stretch of the original route used to transport tobacco from Baltimore west to Frederick. During the Depression, the mills declined and Ellicott City had fallen into disrepair. However, by the early sixties, some visionary Baltimoreans realized the potential of the area and restored those shabby buildings to house upscale shops, pubs, and restaurants. From April through December, the streets teem with people enjoying Ellicott City's quaint shops, excellent food, and western European atmosphere.

As I looked for a parking space, I noticed Harry relaxing on a wooden bench bolted to the mock railroad platform outside the museum. He puffed his cigar and read his newspaper like a passenger awaiting his train.

Although the Museum did not open until ten, only two unoccupied parking spaces remained. I chose the space next to a dilapidated junk heap masquerading as an MGB. The car's faded navy blue body and wire wheels were riddled with rust. It was so infected, I imagined even the floor boards had rotted through. The car's top was down, but its edges were frayed and ragged.

I made the mistake of glancing inside the car as I walked by. The MGB's interior was as ramshackled as its exterior. Had an unhappy raccoon been trapped inside this unfortunate car? Some of the tears in the bucket seats were an inch wide, and years of neglect had rendered the once tan leather dun. The passenger's seat was littered with crumpled MacDonald's bags and Coke cans. The tiny luggage compartment was hidden beneath mounds of manila folders and newspapers. Only a philistine would treat such a fine example of British engineering with such disrespect. My dad had bought me a previously-owned British racing green 1963 MGB when I got my driver's license. Every weekend we cleaned and polished my car.

As I approached the platform, Harry looked up from his paper. He sprang to his feet and waved his arms enthusiastically. I supposed he was worried I might not recognize him. That was highly unlikely considering I spent what seemed like an eternity with him last evening. Harry wore the same rumpled suit sans the soiled tie. I wondered if those were the only clothes he owned.

"Kate, how you doing today?" Harry asked cheerfully, his cigar dangling from the corner of his mouth. Harry appeared quite chipper for a man I assumed had difficulty dragging himself out of bed before noon.

Before I could answer, Harry folded his paper and shoved it under his arm. He took hold of my elbow, and whisked me off the platform and down onto the parking lot. Harry moved swiftly for a portly chain-smoker.

"Considering I am here under protest, rather well. Thank you." We stopped abruptly at the passenger side of my car.

Harry stood between me and the forlorn MGB, and rummaged through his pants pockets. He lost his elbow-grip on his newspaper and it fell, scattering newsprint between the two cars.

While Harry retrieved his paper, I said, "I suppose you want me to drive." Removing my car keys from my shoulder bag, I continued, "That's fine. I would feel safer with me behind the wheel."

Harry rose with an armful of rumbled pages and looked at me as if waiting for instructions for its disposal.

I ignored him and nodded toward the abused MGB, "Look at that poor car, Harry. Only an irreverent fool would let a sports car go to wrack and ruin." Walking around the front of my car, I grumbled, "British cars are like pets. They need lots of love and attention."

I unlocked the doors from the driver's side. Harry did not move. I leaned on the roof and peered at him through the luggage rack. "Harry, do you plan to get into my car sometime in my lifetime?" I pointed at the public facilities to the right of the platform. "Put the newspaper in the receptacle over there and let's get this over with. I have things to do this afternoon."

Harry deposited the newspaper as instructed and returned to the passenger side of my car. We were finally making some progress. Harry eyed me sheepishly as he fumbled in his pants pockets again. Falling cigar ashes decorated his open necked, button-down blue shirt. Harry held up a set of keys and said in a barely audible voice, "I thought we'd go in my car."

For expediency, I decided not to argue. "Fine, where is it?" I tapped my keys on the rack; my eyes fixed on Harry. "Let's not waste any more time playing musical cars."

Harry avoided my gaze. He began to speak then caught himself. He looked away momentarily as if in a quandary. Harry turned back to me, looked me square in the eyes and said resolutely, "My car is right here." Harry bowed like a cavalier; and with a graceful sweeping motion, pointed to the navy blue MGB.

"You must be joking! I am certainly not going to ride or, for that matter, sit in that thing." I could feel my jaw tightening as I turned my back on him. I should have known. No one except Harry Templeton would drive a car that looked like that. If he thinks I'm going to be seen in that car, he is crazy.

Harry sauntered around my station wagon and planted himself directly in front of me. "Now Kate, don't be so persnickety. My car's just a little messy. I've been too busy lately to clean it."

Lately? It must have taken him years to create that. "Harry, my riding in your mobile garbage dump is out of the question. Keep in mind, I am supposed to be playing an enjoyable tennis match." I checked to see if anyone other than Harry was close enough to hear me before I continued. "Make no mistake, Harry Templeton, I am here only because you are blackmailing me."

"Kate, I'm not asking you for hush money," Harry attempted to pacify me by patting my shoulders. "I'm only asking for your time."

"And time is money to me, Harry," I hissed as I shook his hands from my shoulders. "I have wasted money for court time I'm not using. You are costing me money. And that smacks of blackmail to me."

Several people on the parking lot looked our way. Harry leaned toward me. His hair smelled of cigar smoke.

"Kate, be reasonable. I'm not blackmailing you, and you damn well know it. I don't know why, but I feel something dreadful has happened to my friend. And, I just don't know where else to go for help."

"Have you contacted the police in wherever it is your friend lives?"

"Montaview, Pennsylvania. And yes, I contacted them," Harry responded indignantly. "They were absolutely no help." Harry's tone became angry. "In fact, they informed me Roy's reputation as a drunken womanizer led them to believe he was off with some skirt and would return when one of the two of them sobered up."

Harry looked down and shook his head slowly. "That's not the Roy I remember. Sure, he got around in college. But when he graduated then married Marjorie, he settled down. Hell, it wasn't any time before little Rowena was born." Worry covered Harry's face like a veil. "Kate, my gut tells me something awful has happened to Roy."

"All right, Harry," I found myself saying gently. I controlled my momentary urge to touch his hand. "I'll come with you, Harry, but I honestly don't know how much help I'll be."

I nudged Harry toward my passenger door. "You are upset, please let me drive." Not waiting for his reply, I got into my car and turned on the ignition.

Before he opened the passenger door, Harry bent down, looked at me through the open window, and answered softly, "Thanks, Kate."

For the first half hour of our drive, the only sound in the car was the music from my tape, *Tunhuang*. I was familiar with Route 70 west because my maternal great grandmother, Sallie Davis, hailed from Hagerstown. Her family had owned a substantial farm a few miles outside town. According to my mother, the Depression had taken its toll on the Davises, and the family had been forced to sell a large portion of their land.

I remembered our visits to Hagerstown vividly. It seemed as if every time dad passed New Market on Old Route 40, mother would invariably begin her discourse on the

Depression's depletion of her family's fortune. "We were forced to eat margarine instead of butter," she would pout. Then came the tears. "I didn't receive a new dolly every Christmas like most of my friends."

Routinely, my dad reminded her that many families had no food, and that her family was relatively fortunate. Mother disregarded dad's comments and continued whimpering until we turned onto the Davis farm road. As I got older, I concocted feeble excuses for missing those trips. I eventually devised a busy school schedule which conveniently left little time for my parents. I missed many happy hours with my dad, and I felt guilty for forcing him to deal with mother alone. However, he chose to marry her—my relationship with mother was an accident of birth.

I forced my thoughts to return to the matter at hand. I surmised our destination was north of Frederick, but I needed explicit directions. I turned the music down and glanced at Harry. He was slouched—his head turned toward the passenger's window. He must have been entranced by the beauty of the landscape. "Harry, which exit should I take?"

No answer. Harry didn't move.

The Frederick exits were approaching quickly. I reached across and tapped his shoulder. "Harry, I hate to interrupt your meditation, but you need to give me the exit number."

Harry's head jerked from side to side. He appeared startled. He cleared his throat and mumbled something.

I should have known Harry was not enjoying the bucolic setting. He was asleep. I got some satisfaction from confirming Harry doesn't wake til noon.

I bristled, "HARRY . . . wake up, you fool. How do you expect me to drive us to Montaview, if you don't stay awake to give me directions?"

Harry shook and half stretched like a koala bear rising from its nap. He sat upright in his seat.

"Now Kate," he yawned, "the sun was so warm on my face,

and that music was very soothing. Who's that group anyway?"

"Kitaro," I snapped. "Never mind the music. Which exit do I take?

Harry thought a moment. "I think it's exit 52." Harry squinted at the exit signs ahead, his glasses perched on the tip of his nose. "Yeah, Route 15 North, Gettysburg. It's the next one."

Fortunately, I had been hugging the right lane for the last three exits waiting for Harry to return to earth. I whipped off the exit ramp onto Route 15.

"Before you fall asleep again, give me the rest of the directions," I demanded.

"I can't exactly oblige, Kate." Harry looked at me warily. "I don't remember the road names. But, don't you worry your pretty blonde head. I know it has been many years since I was there, but Roy always boasted that things changed very little in Montaview. I'm sure I'll recognize the roads when I see them."

If you could stay awake long enough, I thought. This day was going exactly as I had expected, and I was irritated. To improve my mood, I took a deep breath and exhaled slowly. I turned the stereo's volume up. Kitaro is a New Age musician whose music invariably calms me. The notes seem to align my mind, body and spirit. Those who subscribe to New Age philosophy refer to that alignment as being centered.

My irritation with Harry faded, but I wondered how many times I would need to center myself before my day with Harry Templeton ended.

I thought it wise to establish a more positive line of communication. I glanced over at Harry and said light-heartedly, "I had an odd dream last night about a tall, slender man."

Harry lifted his eyebrows, and his face revealed a renewed interest. "I'm all ears. Tell me, Kate, did you remove your hair band?"

"Save your lecherous thoughts, Harry. I wasn't in the dream. Seriously, though, this man was in front of a grove of hemlocks. As I honed in, I noticed his handsome yet worn face, and strong jaw line. Thick grey hair waved away from his forehead. His eyes were so bloodshot, I could not determine their color; and the skin surrounding them looked puffed. His ample lips were marred by an indentation on the upper right side—probably the result of years of smoking the briarwood pipe in his tweed jacket's vest pocket. His khaki trousers and absinthe turtleneck sweater matched the colors in his jacket perfectly. I sensed his walking stick was merely ornamentation. Actually, I remember thinking his stick was unique but I can't recall why." I attempted to picture the scene in my mind, but found that impossible while driving. "I remember the walking stick's handle formed an angle which was perpendicular to the stick itself. The handle was polished brass, I think, and was shaped like an elongated bullet. I really couldn't recognize what it was. Anyway, I suppose that detail is unimportant. I do recall he looked like a man who kept up appearances. A man who allowed his anxiety to surface only when he was alone. His green Wellingtons were damp with dew. He was the quintessential landed gentry."

"From that description, it sounds like he made quite an impression on you," Harry teased mischievously.

"He was attractive," I admitted. "But it was only a dream, Harry. I'm certain if I had met him somewhere, I wouldn't have forgotten him. However, I must admit, he seemed so real to me I thought, for a moment, I could reach out and touch him."

We rode in silence for several miles. Then, Harry glanced at me and asked, "Did I happen to show you the college photo of Roy I brought with me last night?"

"No. Do you have it now?"

Harry reached into his jacket pocket. "Damn. I must have

forgotten it." Harry shrugged his shoulders. "I tell you, Kate, if I didn't know better, I would swear you were describing Roy. Especially his hair. I was always envious of Roy's mane. He started greying in college, but that made the son-of-a-gun even more attractive to women." As Harry stared out the window, his tone became contemplative. "Roy's face was much like your description. But, his eyes were engaging not blood-shot. That man you described could not have been Roy," Harry said more for his own benefit than mine. "You would have no way of knowing what he looked like. Right?"

"You are absolutely right, Harry. There is no way I could know details about Roy's appearance." I spoke before I thought. "The strangest part of the dream was that I sensed the man was no longer here."

Harry looked puzzled.

I recognized the potential impact of my words and sought others that might be less alarming. But, there were no other words. As Harry stared at me, I felt compelled to say, "Don't ask me why, Harry, but I believe the man in my dream is dead." I chewed on the inside of my lip for a moment. "Let's not jump to any conclusions. There is absolutely no reason to believe Roy is dead." I suddenly felt cold and queasy.

Harry's face turned pallid. He looked away from me. I should not have mentioned my dream.

We rode in silence again. After chastising myself for my thoughtlessness, I contrived to make amends. "Harry, look at those gorgeous mountains in the distance." I babbled, "The rolling hills and pastures are lush this time of year."

No comment. Harry was deep in thought.

An eternity later, Harry spoke, "I think Route 16, Emmitsburg, is the exit we want."

Passing Mt. St. Mary's College must have jogged Harry's memory because he added, "Yes, it's the first exit past the college."

As I turned onto the two-lane road, I saw the gold-domed Shrine of Saint Elizabeth Seton atop the mountain. As a child, I remember my parents' yearly pilgrimages here to pray at the shrine of the first native-born American saint. Feeling constrained by Catholicism, I had refused to acknowledge the solemnity of this place until now.

I was struck by the religious flavor of the tiny college town of Emmitsburg. A church bell rang in the distance. Shops selling religious articles dotted every block. The size and number of Protestant, as well as Catholic, churches amazed me. Another chapel bell pealed. For a mid-summer Saturday afternoon, the streets seemed deserted except for an occasional couple carrying flowers to the Shrine. Bars were conspicuously absent, and all of the restaurants bore innocuous names. Still another church bell rang as we reached the edge of Emmitsburg.

"An odd time to be ringing the church bells, isn't it, Harry."

"I didn't hear any church bells," Harry peered at me. Harry must have been too deep in thought to notice.

Route 16 became a veritable path through a garden of day lilies, tulips, forsythias, and dogwoods once we were outside the town. Harry and I were treated to a fantasia compliments of various birds and insects. The names of the roads leading off the main road all ended in the word Trail. I heard another church bell peal as we passed one particular road. This time I did not bother to inquire whether Harry heard it.

We drove for only a short time before coming upon a thin, rectangular sign announcing the Borough of Montaview, Pennsylvania. An arrow pointed toward Route 116. A banner displaying the Union and Confederate flags hung across the road. The banner read "Civil War Re-Enactments, Montaview, PA August 5-6, & 12-13, Noon till dark".

Harry half-smiled, "The borough sign hasn't changed in

years, a little spruced up maybe. Turn right here. Their drive-way is a few miles up this road just past the golf course."

The narrow road boasted verdant mountains on its left. On its right were pricey chalets overlooking small lakes. The air felt ten degrees cooler and considerably less humid than in Baltimore. For a moment, I was back in Kitzbühel having my first ski lesson. My high school Geography teacher and his wife had organized an excursion to Austria for our senior trip. That had been my first trip abroad, and I had enjoyed it immensely. Funny, I had not thought of that trip in years.

"There's Magic Mountain Golf and Country Club," Harry interrupted my reminiscing. "Looks like they have expanded their operation considerably. Roy mentioned a lot of retirees from Baltimore and D. C. had moved to this area. I suppose the club had to expand to accommodate all the golfers." Harry's scowl hinted he was resistant to change. "Roy's place is coming up on your right."

A tasteful but peeling crest-shaped wooden sign read "Magic Mountain Ski Resort—1489 Summit Trail".

I turned into the entrance. The crumbling blacktop crack-led beneath my tires. A tractor rumbled through a distant pasture. A trace of freshly mown grass sweetened the air. "Roy owns a ski resort?" I wondered why I was surprised that Harry had not mentioned this.

"Not exactly," Harry explained. "The original farm had been in Roy's family for generations. With skiing gaining popularity in the sixties, Roy researched the potential mar-ket. He determined their farm could be a profitable ski re-sort. Roy convinced his parents to convert their farm to Magic Mountain Ski Resort after he finished college. You see, Kate, being the eldest, Roy was expected to assume the role as farm manager. In view of the fact that Roy was quite vocal about his dislike for farming, I suppose his proposition could have been construed as self-serving. His younger brother,

Victor, was adamantly opposed to the resort idea but, as usual, Roy prevailed. Roy and his new bride, Marjorie, moved back to the farm, and he orchestrated the conversion. Then Roy managed the resort and his parents retired. If my memory serves me, Victor was so furious he dropped out of college and moved to the West Coast. I believe he severed all ties with the family."

"Sounds like a case of sibling rivalry to me." I always knew being an only child had its advantages. "I see nothing wrong with Roy's strategic planning and capitalizing on a popular sport."

The road meandered past numerous outbuildings in varying degrees of disrepair. A sign outside a converted stone barn read "Lodge and Restaurant". Surely this was not the ski resort.

"Go past the lodge to the main house, Kate. Roy and his family live there."

I recalled the address here was 1489 Summit Trail as I pulled the car onto the gravel parking pad. Fortunately, it was not 2355 Summit Trail. The numbers two, three, five, and five appeared several times in the dream I had had last night. But after Harry's reaction to my description of the man in that dream, I thought it best not to mention the numbers. Actually, I probably saw those numbers on a spreadsheet at work yesterday; and they reappeared in my dream.

The house was a stately pre-Civil War structure built of the grey stones prevalent in the Gettysburg area. Excepting several cracked window panes, it appeared to have been maintained better than the outbuildings. The extensive gardens surrounding the house were gorgeous, and the stone walkway was heavy with the scent of lavender.

A petite, impeccably groomed, ash blonde woman wearing a Susan Bristol embroidered sweater and matching skirt greeted us at the door. "Well, I declare." She leaned against the door frame and peered at Harry with overly made-up celadon eyes that dwarfed her other features. "Harry Templeton has come to call."

She ushered us through the entrance hall and into the parlor before either of us could respond. "Now, you just sit yourselves down and get comfy while I make you some tea." As she was leaving the parlor, she remarked as an afterthought, "We had to fire our maid a while back. Insubordinate. I certainly will be glad when I can return to Charleston where the help knows its place." She fluttered off.

Harry nodded toward the departing woman. "Roy's wife, Marjorie. She hasn't lost her penchant for clothes or social snobbery." Harry's expression revealed mild disappointment. "As long as I have known her, she has been fantasizing about her triumphant return to her family home in Charleston . . . having conquered the Northern liberals." Harry chortled. "Roy said he wanted a Southern Belle. Well, by God, he got one."

I seized the opportunity to look around in Marjorie's absence. The room was furnished with worn Federal-period antiques. The elaborate window swags were yellowed with age. Indentations in the ancient Persian rugs suggested several large pieces of furniture were missing. A variety of bells were displayed on the tables. There were bells of porcelain, silver, and brass; and they were decorated with everything from hummingbirds to foxes. Crystal vases brimming with myriads of summer flowers were strategically placed throughout the parlor.

"Have the Allnutt's fallen on hard times?"

"Roy didn't mention it to me, but we really haven't kept in touch during the last ten years." Harry removed one of his nasty cigars from his pocket and proceeded to light it. He must have been experiencing cigar withdrawal, knowing better than to smoke in my car. Harry took several puffs, lifted his chin, and blew three smoke rings into the air. "Roy mentioned he wanted to talk to me about finances at our reunion, but I assumed he wanted to compare retirement accounts. Not that I have one."

Marjorie waltzed into the parlor and placed the sterling silver tea service on the highly polished tea table. "I do not care what the temperature, the only appropriate beverage to serve after noon is tea." She ceremoniously arranged the napkins, tea spoons, and stale-looking petit fours. Aunt Pitty Pat would have been proud.

"Harry darling, while I pour, you must introduce me to your lovely lady friend."

Harry and I had not anticipated this. Marjorie was too busy playing hostess to notice his perplexed expression. Harry accepted the tea and napkin, "She, she is . . ."

"His niece." I injected. I not only lied to this woman, I allowed her to think Harry and I were related. God willing, after today, Harry and this entire situation would simply go away.

As I perused the photographs on the mantle, I noticed one of a man who looked miraculously like the man in my dream. I must have been staring because as Marjorie handed me my tea, she commented, "That is my husband, Roy. Still handsome after all these years." Then she sat beside Harry on the white and maroon striped satin settee. In an attempt to disguise my surprise, I turned my attention to my tea cup, "Lovely china, Haviland Tea Rose, I believe. The ladies in my family have always admired that pattern." What am I saying? Harry's family probably used Chinet.

"I forgot my manners," Harry fumbled. "Let me introduce you to my sister's daughter, Kate."

"Katherine," I corrected Harry while looking at the photograph of Roy. "Uncle Harry forgets that I am no longer a child," I grinned as I moved to the window seat beside the fireplace. "And I prefer to be called by my given name."

"Well then," Marjorie patted Harry's hand, "by all means, my dear, we shall certainly endeavor to address you in whatever way you prefer." She fluffed her hair and smoothed her skirt. "Katherine, darling, you may call me Marjorie."

Marjorie did not seem that bad to me.

Marjorie addressed Harry with what appeared to be genuine interest. "Tell me what brings you two all the way up here. Did you come to play golf at the country club next door?"

Considering I could not be sure Harry had recovered from her last question, and neither of us was dressed for golf, I answered, "No, not today. But we wanted to inspect the course for future reference. You see, every month or so, Uncle Harry and I spend a day together . . . golfing or whatever. Usually, we try to get away from the hubbub of the city. So we drove here today to see the golf course. It has an excellent reputation in Baltimore, you know." I sipped my tea to buy time to devise my next move. "When Uncle Harry mentioned his friend, Roy, lived next to our destination, I insisted we stop by." My winning smile preceded my feigned apology, "I hope we aren't interrupting something important."

"Oh my no, Katherine, darling," Marjorie waved her napkin to dissipate either that unpleasant thought or Harry's cigar smoke. "Unfortunately, though, Roy is not at home."

Harry followed my lead casually, "I thought I missed Roy's old Jaguar. Where is he anyway?"

A sumptuous baritone voice from the entrance hall bellowed, "I'll tell you where the son-of-a-bitch is."

"Mark Peale Allnutt, my darling boy. Let's not have our guests think us ungenteel. Now mind your manners and come on in here." Marjorie sprang to her feet and hastened toward that remarkable voice. "This is Mr. Templeton. He's an old friend of your daddy's."

"So I heard," the drop-dead gorgeous, twenty-something year old said as Marjorie lead him into the room.

He gently rested his large hand on her shoulder. Her son towered over her like a protective oak. He, too, bore an uncanny resemblance to the older man in my dream. However, his brown eyes were clear but brooding, and the color of his wavy hair matched his eyes. Mark's khaki safari shorts revealed tanned, muscular legs. His Penn State tee shirt covered his equally muscular chest and shoulders. The sweaty, azure blue bandana around his neck and the leather work boots completed the picture of a man who obviously knew how to work with his hands. If I were a different woman, I would have been in love.

Mark remained standing while Marjorie reclaimed her seat on the settee.

"Now Mark," Marjorie tried cajoling him, "you know you didn't mean one word of what you just said about your daddy. Sit down, darling, and have some tea. Or perhaps you would like to join me in a glass of Savory and James." Marjorie turned to Harry and pursed her lips. "Harvey's Bristol Cream is simply too expensive nowadays. Savory and James tastes very similar, but is half the price." Marjorie flicked at the bottom of her hair. "Lately, I find I need a glass of sherry in the afternoon. It helps my digestion."

Mark's face registered disapproval. Marjorie poured him a cup of tea, then flitted toward the crystal liquor decanters. With resignation, Mark turned his back to his mother as she poured herself a hefty drink.

"What I think of father is no longer of any consequence. Momma please let's change the subject." Mark rested his cup and saucer on a pie-crust table and wiped his forehead with a white, monogrammed handkerchief.

Suddenly, the sound of stampeding bison or, more likely, large dogs filled the entrance hall. As a Belgian Shepherd galloped toward me, Mark reached for his collar but missed. Mark caught the white Shepherd, however, as she sped by.

I am accustomed to large dogs; my dog, Tristan, is a one hundred twenty pound Lab and Shepherd mix. I immediately placed the china out of harm's way and waited for the inevitable. The dog leaped onto my lap, and I was wrestled to the floor. The brass fireplace screen clanged against the brick firewall.

Harry sat dumbfounded.

Marjorie screeched, "Look at those muddy paws! Get those two out of my parlor! What will our guests think?"

After giving his charge the "Sit" command, Mark fell to his knees and tried to separate the tangle of fur and long, blonde hair.

Mark and the white Shepherd joined in when he realized I was laughing hysterically and thoroughly enjoying our romp. At one point in the action, I accidentally rolled on top of Mark. Instinctively, Mark wrapped his arms around me and pulled me closer to him. Our forms fit together with alarming perfection. His body was firm and hot. The smell of his virile sweat and the prickle of his beard stubble were surprisingly enticing. Our eyes locked. Mark eased his mouth into a smile. Embarrassed, I thrust myself away from Mark.

Meanwhile, Marjorie pleaded pitifully for us to stop our roughhousing lest we destroy her remaining family heirlooms. "Mark darling, what have I told you about those dogs?" Marjorie scurried about repositioning each item we had displaced.

Mark gave both dogs the "Down" signal. "Oh, Momma, Charlie and Snowball just wanted to greet Ms . . ." Mark cast me a wry smile. "I'm sorry, I didn't catch your name."

"St. George . . . Katherine St. George." Mark's eyes followed me as I tried to brush the dog hair and mud from my clothes then moved to an inviting wing chair in front of the fireplace. Marjorie's objection to my choice was obvious, but she refrained from asking me to relocate. She mumbled something about, "those dogs always digging, and wouldn't it be prudent to put them back outside while we entertain our guests?" Perceiving Mark's opposition, I said, "I vote the dogs stay here with us. I love animals."

"Well," Marjorie lighted next to Harry and sipped her

sherry, "if you don't mind, Mark really enjoys their company. I do believe, he would rather be around animals than most people." Her irritation subsided, and she winked as Mark cuddled his dogs. "Ever since we adopted those scoundrels from the Antietam Humane Society, the three of them have been inseparable. The poor things. They had been at the shelter for a long time. The shelter personnel tried valiantly to find them homes, as they do with all of their animals. But, at that time, the dogs were already five and six; and no one would adopt them because they were considered too old. Can you imagine?" Marjorie snapped, straightening her shoulders and poking out her chin as if delivering a speech. She took another sip. "People don't understand dogs and cats usually live well into their teens. Even if they didn't have much time left, they give so much unconditional love every moment with them would have been precious." She tempered her indignation. Marjorie did not realize I shared her sentiments. "Anyway, those three are so close, Mark even takes his dogs along while he is working."

Since this was a fact-finding mission, the time was ripe to gather some information. "What kind of work do you do, Mr. Allnutt? Or, may I call you Mark?"

"My Mark is quite an accomplished craftsman," Marjorie chirped proudly, running the perfectly-manicured finger-tips of her right hand across the frayed satin seat. "He makes exquisite furniture and repairs antiques. I will show you the hunt board Mark made me a little later." She sipped her sherry.

If he is so talented, why were their antiques in such poor condition? I wondered.

I thought I saw a blush rise beneath Mark's tan. He glanced at Marjorie, then turned to me but avoided my gaze. "Katherine, I don't stand on pretense, please call me Mark." He sipped his tea. "Momma exaggerates. My woodworking is mediocre. If you want to see real quality craftsmanship, you should see the furniture Uncle Victor creates."

"Victor?" Harry gasped. He echoed my thought.

"Yes, Harry, you remember Roy's brother, Victor, don't you?" Marjorie asked nonchalantly. "About nine years ago . . . now . . . let me get this time frame right. I am terrible with numbers, they just fly right out of my head." She circled her tiny hand above her head as if to demonstrate the numbers leaving her mind. "Yes, I do believe I am correct because it was shortly after Rowena had been diagnosed with diabetes." Marjorie sounded proud she had remembered. "Well anyway, Victor simply appeared one day and announced he had returned to help manage the resort. I must tell you, Victor has been a Godsend to us ever since."

Mark interrupted, "Excuse me, Momma, but I should get back to the mowing. You see, as much as Momma would like to give my job some fancy name, the truth is I am the resident groundskeeper."

I felt slightly disappointed. I did not want Mark to leave for several reasons. First, since Mark obviously disliked his father intensely, I hoped he might inadvertently give us some useful information about Roy's disappearance. And second, I could not believe I was admitting it, even to myself, but I enjoyed looking at him. "So Mark, you are responsible for the lovely gardens? They must be quite time-consuming." I knew from my own experience even a medium-sized garden required beaucoup time.

"They are. But gardening is one of the few passions I allow myself." Mark kissed his mother on her forehead. "It was a pleasure meeting you. Perhaps we will meet again." Mark stared at me and ignored Harry. My neck and face flushed at Mark's provocative suggestion. He sat his cup and saucer on the tea table and left the parlor. I found Mark as attractive from the back as he was from the front. He was the antithesis of the type of man my friends and, most decidedly, my mother, would have thought appropriate.

Marjorie poured herself another sherry. "Don't mind my Mark. He and his daddy had a tiff a few years ago, and Mark, poor baby, harbors a bit of a grudge." Marjorie took a large swallow of sherry. Her speech sounded a bit slurred. "You see, Roy expected his children to follow in his footsteps and manage the family business. Sadly, Mark showed no interest in the business aspects of the resort. Despite that, Roy paid for Mark's first two years at Penn State hoping Mark would come to his senses. When all of Mark's general course work was completed and the time came to declare his major, Mark chose Horticulture instead of Business." Marjorie paused and downed the remainder of her sherry, then patted her mouth daintily with her napkin. "Well," she sighed, "Roy was outraged. He refused to finance Mark's last two years. Mark quit, having no alternative. I was furious with Roy, but I can understand why he did it." Marjorie stared longingly at her empty glass.

She remembered herself and continued, "You see, Mark was Roy's second major disappointment. Roy's precious Rowena," Marjorie turned to Harry and asked, "You remember our first child, Rowena, don't you, Harry?"

"Very well," Harry puffed happily on a newly lit cigar. "Lovely child. In fact, I remember both her and Mark as bright, well-behaved children."

Again, Marjorie walked to the sherry decanter. This time she returned with the decanter in tow. Her expression looked brittle as if her face would crack with her next word. "Well, Roy's little Miss Perfect took her Business degree from Mt. St. Mary's. Then the headstrong child turned her back on our business and pursued her artistic endeavors." Marjorie added grudgingly, "I must admit she has always been quite artistic. But, Rowena was such a daddy's girl, I assumed she would follow in Roy's footsteps." Marjorie poured another sherry, drank half, then added incredulously, "She used her inheritance from her Grandmomma to buy an art gallery here in town," Marjorie grumbled as she perched unsteadily on the edge of the settee. "That silly girl actually thinks she will be able to make a living with her art. She will soon learn success in the art world depends on much more than talent."

I drink very little, but from Marjorie's fish-eyed stare, I surmised we should discuss Roy's absence with Marjorie before she became totally drunk. Harry seized the reins while I considered my next line of questioning. From Harry's own addiction, he must have known we had precious little time before Marjorie would succumb.

Harry's inflection was resolute. "As I mentioned before, Marjorie, I did not see Roy's old Jaguar parked outside. I can't imagine Roy sold it. That car was his prized possession. So, where is the Jaguar and where is Roy?"

Marjorie tilted her head toward Harry and blinked her huge, vacant eyes numerous times. She appeared to be attempting to bring Harry's face into focus. "To be honest, Harry, I don't know. Roy simply went out for one of his usual evening walks, and didn't return." Marjorie reached for the decanter.

"Didn't you find that strange?" I asked.

"No, Katherine, Roy often disappears for days." Marjorie concentrated on her drink. "He developed that annoying little habit years ago." Marjorie gulped her drink. "Mark assures me his daddy just needs some time alone to contemplate the state of the world or something to that effect." Marjorie fingered several strands of her hair and pouted. "I just wish Roy would have waited to disappear until after he signed the sales contract."

"Sales contract?" Harry and I sang a duet.

"Yes, Magic Mountain Golf and Country Club wants to buy our place so they can expand. Their development corporation has been after us for years to sell, but until last month Roy steadfastly refused."

"What changed his mind?" I asked as I walked toward the window at the far end of the parlor. Mark was not in sight.

"I have no clue." Marjorie answered as she poured another drink. "I had pleaded with him for years to sell so I—I mean—we could move to Charleston to a proper house. This resort has been a losing proposition from the start. But you know Roy." Marjorie looked to Harry for affirmation. "He is so obstinate, he would not admit he had made a mistake. About six weeks ago, for some reason Roy announced he was seriously considering selling. He asked Elliot, our family lawyer and Rowena's fiancé, to draw up a sales contract." Marjorie's head rocked from side to side as she stared blankly at her napkin. "Naturally, Elliot responded immediately, and we have been waiting for Roy to sign ever since."

I needed clarification, "So you mean you and this person, Elliot, were waiting for your husband to sign?"

"Lord no. Not Elliot." Marjorie seemed surprised by my question. "Elliot has never been in favor of the sale. To the contrary, each time the family tried to persuade Roy to sell, Elliott backed Roy's refusal one hundred per cent." She paused, "Elliot agrees with Roy on everything. He is Roy's most loyal supporter. And don't think Roy doesn't appreciate that. He treats Elliot like a son. The son Roy always wanted. My poor Mark." She sighed and shrugged her shoulders. "He could not or would not conform to his daddy's expectations."

Marjorie fanned herself with her napkin and rubbed her right temple. "I feel a headache coming on. It must be this damned heat." Her hand flew over her mouth as if to stop another ungenteel word from escaping. She sat her unfinished drink on the tea table. As she rose, her linen napkin fell to the floor. Marjorie stepped on it as she listed to the left. "If you two will excuse me, I must lie down." Marjorie staggered into the entrance hall and grasped the newel post.

"Have a walk around the grounds. They are lovely this time of year. If you can find your way to the woods, we have a magical pond. Katherine might like to see the swans."

Harry and I hurried to the hall to help her up the stairs, but Marjorie insisted she could navigate. We watched as she mounted each step unsteadily. When she finally reached the top, Marjorie called over her shoulder, "Roy will come home when he's ready. He always has." She took several shaky steps then stopped and looked over the banister at Harry and me. "Strange, this was the first time Roy took his walking stick with him."

The air outside was humid and smelled of rain. I wanted Harry to get this show on the road. I thought Marjorie's explanation for Roy's absence was plausible, and hoped Harry did also. If we left now, we could miss the storm that darkened the sky to the west. And, I would be home in time to go riding in the indoor ring later this evening.

As we approached my car, Harry suggested we snoop around a little before heading back to Baltimore. He grabbed my elbow and escorted me in the direction of the outbuildings before I could object.

Harry remarked, "Call me crazy, but this whole thing doesn't feel right."

My tolerance was waning, and it must have shown. Harry offered quickly, "Look Kate, humor me today, and I won't bother you again." Harry held his right hand up as if on the witness stand, "I promise."

Hallelujah! Harry will finally go away. With that happy prospect in mind, what is an hour or two? "You have a deal, Harry." I clapped my left palm against Harry's already raised right. We laughed like two naughty children. Strange, I could not remember the last time I did anything like that.

Like the main house, the lodge's landscaping was perfect. The steep-pitched, tin roof was unfortunately in need of repair. The window frames were warped and peeling, and the grey stone needed repointing. Harry tried the Dutch door, but it would not budge.

I was relieved. I find it inappropriate to enter someone else's property uninvited. Harry obviously held no such objection. Harry investigated the perimeter by wandering among the ewes and boxwoods, and trampling the day lilies.

"Kate," Harry motioned for me to join him. "Look in this window and tell me if you see anything suspicious."

"What are you planning to do while I do that?"

"Don't worry, Kate, I will be on the other side of the lodge doing exactly the same thing. Call if you discover anything." Harry vanished around the corner.

Storm clouds blew toward the mountain, and the wind soughed through the trees. While peering through the dirty windows, I felt an inexplicable urge to look behind me.

The lodge's interior was cavernous, and the numerous but small windows provided insufficient light. White sheets covered everything on the muted floor. The lodge reminded me of a sepulcher. I trembled. I told myself my reaction was ridiculous. I breathed deeply and focused on the interior. Despite my concentration, I could identify nothing. How was I to determine whether anything was suspicious?

Suddenly, something cold brushed against my bare arm. I shrieked as my left forearm connected with someone's ribs.

An all too familiar voice cried out, "Damn it, Kate!" I whirled around in time to see Harry doubling over in pain. He hugged his torso tightly. "What the hell are you trying to do—kill me?"

I hadn't thought of that. "No, I am not trying to kill you, you fool." My heart pounded. "You scared me. Why did you sneak up on me?"

"Sneak up on you? How could this body sneak up on anyone?" Harry winced. "Unless, of course, you're deaf."

"No need to be sarcastic, Harry," I huffed, as I helped Harry to a wrought iron bench beneath a willow. "Take several deep breaths. You will feel better." I felt slightly guilty for inflicting such pain on Harry. The operative word here is slightly.

For a few blessed minutes, we sat in silence. This beautiful setting had a calming effect. Harry reached inside his jacket and gingerly stroked his ribs. He straightened up finally. "For a thin woman, you carry quite a wallop. You could have broken my ribs." Harry patted the vest pocket of his suit jacket. "Damn, Kate, I'll bet you broke my cigars."

"Never mind your cigars." Harry could be quite amusing at times. "Did you discover anything suspicious?"

"No. But there was no light." Anticipation etched his brow. "Did you?"

"No. How could I see anything if you couldn't?" I should have know where my question would lead.

"Well, Kate, you can . . . you know, *see* things other people can't." Harry squirmed. "I hoped you might be able to *see* something."

"I am not a magician, Harry. Anyway, I do not think there is anything suspicious to see. I am certain Marjorie knows her husband better than anyone. She seemed confident Roy would return soon." I rose and walked briskly toward my car, calling back to Harry, "And I believe her."

I found it difficult to imagine, but Harry caught up to me and stepped into my path. He held up both his chubby hands like a school crossing guard. "Did you notice Mark watching us from the ridge?"

My gesture indicated I had not, but my interest was piqued. Harry continued, "Mark stopped mowing and watched us from his tractor at first." Harry pointed to what I assumed was the beginner ski slope. "Then, Mark abandoned his tractor and climbed that hill."

I pushed his arm down. "You fool. If Mark is watching us, do you want him to know we are discussing him?" I squinted in the direction Harry had pointed. "Someone is standing on the ridge, but it could be anyone. No, I believe you are right. I can see Mark's dogs."

"See! See! I told you," Harry's eyes danced with excitement.

"Mark lives here. He has a right to be anywhere he pleases. You forget, we are the ones who are trespassing." I had reached my limit. "I simply do not see what relevance . . ."

Harry interrupted. "Kate, the relevance is that Mark said he needed to finish mowing. Take a look. Has he finished?" Harry spread his arms and circled around as if to encompass the entire resort. "No." Harry poked his index finger into my shoulder, "I am telling you, he is keeping an eye on us for some reason."

I shoved Harry's hand aside. "And the reason is we are two strangers wandering around his family's property peering into windows. I have seen enough. Let's go."

Harry grasped my shoulders squarely and looked directly into my eyes the way a parent does when he wants to hold his child's attention. "Kate, we have just begun checking things out. Look, you promised to humor me," he said earnestly. "And I say you owe me at least one quick turn around the grounds."

Arguing would have been futile. Harry wanted a quick turn around the grounds? That was exactly what he got. I marched begrudgingly through the herb garden, the garage, several implement sheds, the grey wooden barn, and the stone spring house. Harry followed a safe distance behind. Storm clouds billowed overhead, and the air was bracing. But the rain never came.

As we tramped about, Mark changed vantage points accordingly. Mark never lost sight of us or us of him. I maintained my pace as we traipsed through pastures and traversed slopes even though Harry lagged farther and farther behind. Harry's out-of-shape body finally proved the instrument of my revenge.

Harry stopped abruptly at the base of the third slope, and wailed, "I'm dead tired!" I looked back to see him flopped on the grass panting. "Every inch of my body hurts." He massaged his legs and conceded. "You win, Kate, we can head home."

I stood akimbo over Harry and reveled in my victory. I shivered from the cool, damp air. Harry struggled to get up and remove his suit jacket. He ignored my resistance as he wrapped his jacket around my shoulders.

Since I had endured all of Harry's nonsense, I believed I deserved to gain some pleasure from this day. "We are so close to the pond, could we see the swans?" My childlike tone annoyed me.

"Sure, Kate," Harry beamed, my petulance forgiven. "All-in-all, you have been a good sport. We can do anything you want."

The metallic sun pierced the tenebrous, evening sky. The hemlock grove was the perfect background for the magical pond. A swan and her cygnets shimmered on the pond's surface. The mother ignored our intrusion as she nuzzled and preened her babies.

Harry and I sat on the bank and reviewed our findings. He reluctantly admitted that since we had uncovered nothing truly suspicious, his dreadful feeling about Roy was probably indigestion resulting from his poor diet. As Marjorie had assured us, Roy would probably return soon. Harry thanked me for my help and jovially granted me my freedom. My secret would be safe with him. For some inexplicable reason, I believed him.

We lingered by the pond, savoring its serenity. Rosemary and lemon verbena from our trek through the herb garden scented our clothes. The swans' ballet was unrivaled by any human performance. Marjorie was right. This pond was magical.

Suddenly, my eyes began to blur, and the scene changed.

Cloaked in a mist, I thought I saw two figures emerging from the hemlocks. One was short and stocky. The other was tall and slender. Their posture and movements appeared hostile, but I heard only the night sounds of the pond. The taller figure eventually turned and stalked away dropping a long, thin object as it left. In its haste, it did not stop to retrieve the object.

The shorter figure bellowed, but the other continued walking. Again, I could hear no words. The shorter figure was apparently enraged because it swooped down, retrieved the dropped object then ran after the other. The distance between them closed in an instant. The shorter figure yanked the other to attention. Grappling ensued. The shorter figure suddenly raised the long, thin object and struck the other. A sharp pain pierced my forehead. I winced and grabbed my head.

The victim reeled from the blow, staggered, then fell beside the pond. The assailant dropped the bludgeon and rushed to the victim's side. I clasped my hands over my tightly closed eyes and hoped that might make the horror vanish. My pain was so intense, I felt faint. When I opened my eyes, everything was a blur. I saw only the pond and swans when my vision cleared. The two figures had vanished.

Harry must have been roused by my strange and sudden actions. "Kate? What the hell's wrong? You look terrible." Harry steadied me.

The pain was still unbearable, and I cupped my hands around my head. "It's a headache, Harry. That's all. I need to go home."

I was grateful to Harry for helping me to my feet. As we walked slowly to my car, Harry asked, "Can I drive you home? You don't look like you are in any shape to drive."

"Thank you, Harry, I would appreciate that."

Chapter 5

Early Sunday morning I awoke from a dream so frightening I clung to my pillow for security. Sweat soaked my cotton nightgown and bed linens. Still dazed, I looked around my bedroom. The sight of my furry bunkmates sleeping on the bottom of the bed reassured me I was, in fact, safe.

I reached for the telephone on my night stand. I dialed 411. "The telephone number for Harry Templeton, please." I ignored my vow that once I was finally rid of that pesky reporter, I would never speak his name again. I needed to talk to Harry immediately. I dialed the number the operator gave me.

The telephone rang several times. No answer. No answering machine.

Five rings later, someone lifted the receiver, yawned then fumbled with the phone. I heard the ping of what sounded like an alarm clock hitting the floor. A gravelly voice shouted, "It's seven a.m. Who the hell is this?"

"Harry, it's me, Kate." I breathed deeply and collected my thoughts. "I want to return to Roy's home today. And, I want you to come with me."

"I must still be dreaming." Muffled background noise sounded like he was trying to prop himself up. I heard Harry puffing and knew he had lit a cigar. "Kate, you were so unhappy about my forcing you to go to the Allnutt place yesterday, why would you want to go back there today?" Harry finally remembered his manners, "By the way, how's your headache?"

"It is gone, thank you." I swallowed hard, trying to muster the courage to focus on my dream. "I had a horrible dream last night." I paused, and petted my cat, Gareth. "On second thought, it was not a dream. It was a nightmare." My voice cracked, "I think it took place at Roy Allnutt's pond."

Harry attempted to assuage my fear, "Kate, calm down." Harry puffed. "You probably dreamed about the pond because we were just there." Harry sneezed, then blew his nose. "Sorry about that." Harry cleared his throat, then continued. "If you remember, that is where your headache suddenly came on. That's all. Don't worry your pretty head about it."

"No, Harry," I insisted. "There is something dreadfully wrong. I can feel it."

"Do you want to talk about it?" Harry sounded more co-herent.

"No," I stated emphatically, "I want to return to the pond so I can try to make sense of my dream. Perhaps the whole thing will become clearer if I stand where I believe it took place." I waited for his response, but heard only puffing. "You were the one who got me involved in this." I should have been embarrassed by my puerility. "I intend to go to Magic Mountain Lodge this morning. Are you coming with me or not?"

Harry teased, "We can't have you traipsing all over Roy's place alone now can we? That hunk, Mark, might find you snooping around one of the barns, and who knows what might happen."

We agreed to meet at 9:30 sharp at the Railroad Museum. Ever cautious, I thought it unwise to have Harry come to my home. Our trip would hopefully convince me my feelings were nothing more than an overactive imagination brought on by a lack of food and that awful headache. If that was the case, I would never see Harry Templeton again and I could see no reason why I should invite him into my home.

I had a great deal to accomplish before meeting Harry. First, I performed my daily pet chores. My motley crew stared grudgingly when I fed them then failed to spend my normal Sunday morning hour or so lulling around the house showering them with my undivided attention.

Having no idea how long I would be gone, I rang my wonderful housekeeper, Mrs. Huziej, to ask her to look in on the crew around five p.m., and feed them if they appeared to be hungry. I was certain they would play on her sympathy as they always do. She explains in her heavy Hungarian accent how "they looked up at me so pitifully, I had to give them treats." I mentioned my sweaty bed linens, and she offered to launder them. Bless her heart. I hoped she would not wonder why the sheets were in that condition. Mrs. Huziej was truly a treasure. She adored my pets and they adored her. Plus, she kept my home spotless.

Second, I needed to have someone exercise my horse, Flute. I knew I could call either of my friends, Marcia or Susan, and they would oblige. We three board our horses at Periwinkle Farm. After my Saturday morning tennis match with Ric, I usually spend the remainder of my weekend with my friends at Periwinkle. Marcia, Susan, and I met there four years ago and began transporting our horses to shows together. Out of our mutual love for our horses and, in fact, all creatures, we have developed a bond of friendship and admiration for one another that sometimes makes me wonder if we had shared other lifetimes. Our connection is so profound, I sometimes entertain the possibility of reincarnation. Strangely, we have often been mistaken for sisters.

Marcia did not answer when I rang. Susan was at home, fortunately, and agreed without hesitation to exercise Flute. Susan said she groomed her horse, Karma, yesterday, and offered to groom Flute for me after their ride. I accepted appreciatively.

My most important concerns resolved, I finally called Ric to advise him I could not make our tennis match and why. Ric needled me unmercifully about Harry, then accepted my absence with a devilish caveat, "I have it on good authority fleshy, cigar-smoking reporters are terrors in the woods. Call me when you get home. I can't wait to hear what you discover."

When I arrived, Harry was waiting beside his rattle trap in wrinkled dress slacks and a dingy white oxford shirt with the sleeves rolled up. His hair was still damp from his shower and reminded me of a rooster's topknot. Didn't Harry own a comb? At this early hour, he already reeked of cigars. Yet, I felt somehow relieved to see him.

Harry did not mention going in his car. We agreed Harry should drive my car so I could concentrate on my dream and not worry about traffic. Harry retrieved something from the front seat of his car as I buckled myself into the passenger seat. He squeezed himself into the driver's seat while balancing a cardboard tray containing two covered, styrofoam cups. The smell of piping hot coffee filled the car and reinforced the heat and humidity the air conditioner had been working hard to offset.

"Here you go, Kate, black coffee." He rested the tray on the emergency brake lever. Harry handed me a cup.

"Thank you, no. I don't drink coffee." My hand parroted my words.

"You do now," Harry asserted, as he shoved the coffee into my hand. "You look like a zombie. Coffee is just what the doctor ordered."

I was not up to arguing and thought perhaps caffeine might jolt me from my stuporous state. Fear had awakened me so abruptly from that awful nightmare, I was not my usual alert self. I sipped the coffee and settled in for the long ride to Montaview, Pennsylvania. "Thank you, Harry." He smiled sagaciously.

We drank our coffee silently until we reached Frederick. Then we chatted about the stifling summer, the excellent condition of my Volvo despite its advancing age, the strength of its air conditioner, and the relative quality of store-brewed coffee. We scrupulously avoided addressing my nightmare. Because I was unwilling to discuss it on the telephone, Harry was afraid to irritate me by mentioning it again.

I picked at my cup's plastic top as we drove through Emmitsburg. Finally, I said, "I hate to admit this, Harry, but now I feel foolish insisting we drive up here today. You were right to suggest my nightmare was nothing more than the result of my horrible headache."

"I don't know much about you, Kate." Harry's eyes remained focused on the road. He chuckled. "You are certainly tough to get to know." Harry tossed me a sly glance. "But, having been around you even briefly, I do know you are not a rash person. And given your gift, we would be foolish if we didn't check it out."

I sighed in relief and felt free to relax and admire the sumptuous scenery. As the beauty of the countryside and the warmth of the sun lulled me, I considered Harry's comment about my being "tough to get to know". I have always considered myself a discerning person. I carefully select those I allow to truly know me. Harry is not going to be one of them unless something drastic happens to change my mind. Although, he is not quite as bad as I first thought.

Along Route 16, between Emmitsburg and the turnoff for Montaview, I heard church bells peal. A tremulous feeling overcame me as I wondered if it was the same place where I had heard them yesterday. I chewed my lip and peeked at Harry out of the corner of my eye. He concentrated on the road and his expression remained unchanged. If Harry had not heard the bells, he might think I was weird—hearing nonexistent bells twice in two days. I decided not to mention them. Besides, Emmitsburg was a parochial town. The ringing surely emanated from one of its churches.

I flicked my fingernail against my bottom teeth. Church bells ringing at eleven-fifteen on Sunday morning seemed odd. Masses were usually said on the hour, and Protestant services were held earlier. I had absented myself from the Catholic church for so many years; however, I might be mistaken about the mass times.

Harry asked warily as he turned onto Route 116, "Can we talk about your nightmare now?"

"Harry, we are so close to Roy's pond, let's wait until we get there." I begged his indulgence for a short while longer. "If I see or feel nothing once I am at the pond, then we can return to Baltimore. I will be able to forget my nightmare just as I would a frightening movie." As an afterthought, I offered, "I will, of course, buy you lunch along the way for your trouble."

"Now you are acting foolish," Harry bristled. "I won't have a woman buy me lunch or anything else for that matter!"

Harry was truly a dinosaur. We turned into the entrance to Magic Mountain Lodge; Harry and I had no time to squabble about lunch.

Not more than twenty yards down the road, Harry swerved my Volvo onto the grass and stopped directly in front of a placard that read, "TODAY—Civil War Re-enactment—139th Pennsylvania Infantry & 7th Tennessee Company A".

Harry and I stared at the placard, then at one another. We saw no evidence of activity of any kind.

My brow wrinkled. "I wonder why Marjorie and Mark failed to mention this to us yesterday?"

Harry's expression made his reply obvious. "They didn't mention it because they didn't want us to know." Harry 's ruddy cheeks turned scarlet as he pounded his palms on the steering wheel. "They do not want us around here asking questions. That's why."

At least Harry and I had one thing in common—we detested being duped.

"I know this is a change in plans, but I say we attend that re-enactment. Maybe we will discover why the Allnutts don't want us around." I felt my jaw tightening. "We might be able to walk around the pond unnoticed if there is a crowd."

Harry added as he threw my car in reverse, "And, if we get lucky, Kate, my beauty, we might meet some of the locals. I hope they can shed some light on Roy's disappearance." My old Volvo raced toward the lodge raising a trail of dust that was probably visible from Route 116.

As we rounded a curve, a maroon Jaguar XKE convertible sped past us and headed toward the resort's entrance. The top was up; but the driver appeared to be dark haired with a shadowy mark on his or her forehead. I chose not to mention this image to Harry because, as usual, I saw it in my mind.

I was surprised to see cars and vans lining both sides of the lane when we passed the first group of outbuildings. Many bore bumper stickers reading "Re-enactors do it with a bang!" and "Re-enactments—Living Histories of the Civil War". Vehicles covered the parking lot and the pasture.

I remarked as I attempted to put the vision of the Jaguar out of my mind, "I had no idea these things were so popular." I unbuckled my seat belt.

"Hell yes, Kate. Anything pertaining to the Civil War is extremely popular. Don't you do anything except work and ride horses?"

"Excuse me." I lifted my right eyebrow and assumed a wry expression. "How did you know I rode?"

"Your friend, Ric, told me Friday night while you were in the powder room. Besides, he also mentioned it when I teased you about eating pizza with a knife and fork. Remember?"

Powder room? I had not heard those words in years. Ric,

huh? What right had he to reveal the intimacies of my life to Harry Templeton?

Harry backed my station wagon under a mammoth oak, then said, "Don't give me that look. The car will stay cooler here." Harry deposited his empty styrofoam cup into the trash bag I held out to him. He noted, "With your car in this position, if anyone gets too nosey about why we are here, we can make a quick get away." Harry nodded his head in self-acknowledgment of his strategic brilliance.

We stepped out of my car and into the 1860s. The re-enactors and some of the spectators wore period costumes. Harry and I threaded through clusters of soldiers in uniforms of both indigo and grey wool. The heat was so intense even in the mountains many of them had already removed their heavy jackets revealing linen or cotton shirts under their suspenders. Those portraying gentlemen wore vests. Accouterments such as cap boxes or bayonets were attached to the re-enactors' leather belts. The officers alone carried pistols in their belts.

Women clothed in long cotton dresses complete with hoops prudently removed their hats and day caps, and observed their men's maneuvers from under the shade trees.

Harry and I blended in with the majority of the audience as we made our way to the pond. We were within twenty feet of its edge when a well-rehearsed male voice came over the resort's public address system. "Ladies and gentlemen. Magic Mountain Lodge welcomes one and all to this Civil War re-enactment featuring company drills, a parade and, later this afternoon, a tactical between the 7th Tennessee Company A and the 139th Pennsylvania Infantry."

The words reverberated between a speaker behind me and a new, luxurious maroon Jaguar XJS convertible directly in my path. A man in his early thirties, microphone in hand, stood in the Jag's rear seat and continued addressing the crowd. "For your convenience, sutlers and food stands are located near the lodge. The first set of drills will commence in about fifteen minutes." The announcer surveyed his audience, then concluded, "This is Elliott Danforth of the law firm of Billings and Newkirk, P.A., your proud sponsor of this event. Enjoy this exciting day! Thank you."

Still basking in the spotlight, the speaker vaulted from the Jaguar's rear seat and strutted towards his waiting admirers. Or, perhaps that was merely my perception.

I poked Harry's side with my elbow, "So *that* is Elliott Danforth." My mind clicked back to our conversation with Marjorie. Harry's mien hinted he did not remember the name. I quipped, "Harry, you fool, yesterday Marjorie described Elliott Danforth as their family lawyer and Rowena's fiancé." My lack of rest and my proclivity for intolerance caused me to blast Harry, "Were both Marjorie and you imbibing yesterday?"

Perspiration beaded Harry's forehead and cascaded down his neck. He wiped both with a crumpled tissue. "I told you, Kate. I don't drink anymore." His tone sounded miffed, and he tightened his fists.

I believe Harry might have swung at me if I had been a man. I instinctively protected my face with my hands, "Okay, okay!! I was totally out of line, Harry. I am sorry."

Harry stared me in the face. He eyes were those of a wounded soldier. Guilt stabbed me like a bayonet. My countenance begged forgiveness. But this time, Harry did not pardon me magnanimously or replace his frown with his typical jovial mask. His stare held me well into the next century. Harry turned from me without a word, and walked toward the crowd surrounding Elliott. I followed him like a repentant child.

I pretended my words were my mother's whenever I lashed out cruelly. But, upon reflection, I confessed they were mine. At those times, I am relieved I am childless.

I watched Elliott perform as Harry and I made our way to

the front of Elliott's entourage. I would have taken Elliott for a laborer except for his Brooks Brothers navy polo shirt and chinos. He was built like a construction worker—average height and stocky. Elliott had close-cropped, medium brown curls, several of which bounced onto the middle of his wide forehead despite his bulky fingers' efforts to comb the aberrant locks backward. In the glary sunlight, Elliott's eyes matched his polo shirt. Was that mere coincidence? His duck-bill mouth, probably the result of habitual thumb sucking as a child, rendered his otherwise pedestrian face memorable. It appeared what Elliott lacked in looks, he made up for in personality. The crowd hung on his every word.

I whispered in Harry's ear contritely, "I have a suggestion, Harry." His eyes fixed on Elliott, Harry nodded for me to continue. "Why not stay for a while and listen to what Elliott has to say while he is holding court? We might glean some information that could be helpful."

Harry did not answer, but folded his arms across his chest and cocked out his left hip. I assumed that meant we were staying. Elliott was discussing antique firearms. He mentioned that during the Civil War, the government issue rifles were either American Springfield or British Enfield. He demonstrated how to load a black powder weapon. Elliott assured his audience that, for safety reasons, live cartridges were never used during re-enactments. Someone asked if those weapons belonged to him. Elliott answered that they did, and he boasted that he had both designed and built a cherry gun cabinet to display his treasures. Oddly, I could have sworn I heard a band saw somewhere in the background.

A teenaged boy asked why Elliott was not participating in the re-enactment. That question had crossed my mind too. Elliott explained that he had joined the 139th Pennsylvania Infantry but, to date, had been so busy with his law practice he had been unable to attend any meetings or practice drills. I got the distinct feeling, however, Elliott was the type who enjoyed the trappings of the re-enactors, but could not be bothered to devote any quality time to the group. He looked more like a golfer to me. My ex-husband loved to sail but spent most of his weekends on the golf course courting potential clients. I presumed Elliott assessed that golfers made better business contacts than re-enactors. Frankly, the business woman in me could not fault Elliott for that.

I meekly suggested we walk around the pond since I did not see how Elliott's discussion of Civil War firearms could yield any significant information about Roy. Harry still was not talking to me, but lead me out of the crowd and toward our original destination.

With the first drill about to begin, the throng left Harry and me to go about our task undisturbed. I proceeded slowly around the pond's perimeter being careful not to frighten the swans. I walked among the creatively planted ewes and ornamental hollies because I wanted to feel the pond's heart-beat. Harry watched my movements from a wrought iron bench in the hemlocks' shadows. He must have sensed I needed to be alone.

I sat in the newly mown grass in approximately the same spot where Harry and I had rested last evening when I thought I had envisioned the two figures. The grass felt soft and warm against my forearms as I leaned back on my elbows. My hands massaged the summer earth as I closed my eyes and bent my neck backward, catching the sun's rays on my face. I cleared my mind and provided the empty stage for whatever the universe was about to present to me. I felt apprehensive. The scene of the quarrel between the two misty figures played out as it had last night, but this time, with more intensity. I began to feel queasy. The sound of a pulsating heart assaulted my ears. The short figure once again swung the long thin object and it struck the tall figure's head. My hands instinctively clenched the ground. The scene kept repeating. My mind was consumed by it. My hands tore out mounds of grass as I fought the pain in my head and my increasing horror. I realized I was feeling exactly what the victim had felt.

Between the throbs of pain, I heard a distant voice calling, "Kate . . . Kate what's wrong?" Strong hands grasped my shoulders and gently, rhythmically shook my upper body then laid me face up on the ground. I thought I smelled wood burning. "Kate, come on now. You're scaring me. Please . . . please wake up!"

The smell became stronger. I finally forced my eyes open and saw Harry bending over me shielding my face from the sun.

Harry brushed a damp lock of hair from my face then cupped my cheeks in his hands. Worry distorted his moon face as he asked. "Are you okay?"

I nodded.

Harry bent closer and whispered, "What happened to you?"

I gasped, "It was the same vision I had at this pond last night." I clamped my eyes shut as the scene raced through my mind once more. Every cell in my body screamed. I must get away from this terrible place. I bolted up, inadvertently pushing Harry aside. As I sat on the ground, staring into nothingness, I heard myself say, "In my mind I saw what looked like two people fighting." I interlocked my fingers over my heart. "One struck the other with a long thin object, and . . . and," my bottom lip began to quiver, "I think the victim is dead!"

Harry pulled me to him and held me tightly. My emotions threatened to control me. That scene had been so disturbing, I felt tears welling. Not tears of fear but tears of rage. I had witnessed a brutal murder and had done nothing to prevent it. But, it had already happened; there was nothing I could have done. My rational side was satisfied. My emotional side was not. I inhaled deeply and finally calmed myself, but the uneasy feeling in the pit of my stomach would not leave me. I realized suddenly I was as rigid as a mannequin in Harry's arms. Why couldn't I respond to his unconditional concern? I sat silently while the radiant sunlight cleansed and renewed me.

Harry said eventually, "Let's get away from here so you can tell me exactly what you saw." Harry released his hold on me and heaved his bulk up. He held both his hands out to me. I welcomed his help. When I was on my feet and steady, Harry put his arm around my shoulder and guided me toward the wrought iron bench.

Apprehension besieged me again as we made our way around the pond. I began to feel like I was being sucked down into a quagmire when we reached the place where, in my vision, the victim had fallen to the ground. I stopped on the spongy grass in the shadow of the hemlocks, and felt unable to move. I began to feel weak. I shut my eyes immediately, and attempted to visualize myself standing straight and tall. However, in my mind, I saw the victim's limp body being pushed into a hole. Mud began raining down onto the prone body. I felt silt slapping against my skin. I saw mud ooze into the gaping mouth. My throat felt obstructed. I saw mud plug the nostrils. I could not breathe. I saw mud weighing down the eyelids. I could not open my eyes. My world was dark. I was smothering. I knew mud had been the victim's sarcophagus.

I forced my eyes open. I had no idea how much time had passed. I felt the sensation of cool metal against my bare arms. I realized I was sitting on the wrought iron bench in the shade of the hemlocks. A stranger knelt at my feet and held both my hands in his. I snatched my hands from him and wondered aloud, "Where is Harry?"

Harry's finger tips tapped the back of my shoulders reassuringly. "I'm right here, Kate, my beauty." His tone sounded strained, artificial. Harry walked around the bench. "I was just telling Mr. Danforth here that one of your migraines must have come on you suddenly. And that's why you were acting so strangely." Harry stopped directly behind the kneeling man. Harry contorted his face to attract my attention. He shook his head and waved his right hand signaling me to offer nothing more.

The other man rose and joined me on the bench. I must have been so bewildered, I still did not recognize him.

The man took my hands again and held them in his. His wide hands felt smooth, feminine. But the energy emanating from his hands was electric. I noticed his nails were manicured and covered with clear polish. I raised my eyes from his hands and caught his gaze. His eyes reflected anxiety. I recognized his voice as he said, "Ms. St. George, I am Elliott Danforth. Are you feeling better?" He continued before I could answer. "I was watching the drill when I observed your . . . how should I put this . . . rather erratic behavior. I ran over to see if I could be of any assistance."

At this distance, his cascading curls, indigo eyes, and pursed lips made me reassess his looks. All Elliott Danforth needed was a bow around his neck, and he would have been teddy-bear cute.

Harry asked whether I felt well enough to walk to the car. I answered "yes", and Harry offered some lame excuse about needing to return to Baltimore immediately. He thanked Elliott for his concern, and practically lifted me from the bench. We left Elliott sitting alone on the bench looking somewhat surprised.

Harry declared after we were out of earshot, "We are getting the hell out of here before something else happens to you."

"I 'm feeling better now, Harry. And when I tell you what I experienced back there, you will be as certain as I am that we are onto something."

Harry bought us iced teas, and we leaned against my car. I related my latest vision to him in an undertone—detail by horrific detail. Harry's eyes widened more with each word. He forgot to puff his recently lit cigar. Harry removed his glasses and tapped them against his pant leg as I spoke. The more ghastly the detail, the harder he tapped.

Harry chewed his cigar like a baby chewed a teething ring. After I finished my descriptions, Harry said, "So, what you are telling me, Kate, is that you feel someone is buried beside that pond."

"Correct." I bit my bottom lip while searching for the right words. "Harry, I am sorry to say this, but I feel that someone could very well be your friend, Roy."

Harry answered with resignation, "I think we should advise the local police."

I laughed sardonically. "Right, Harry. What should we tell them? That I happened to see someone I thought might be Roy murdered, then buried in a hole beside the pond. And, to add even more credence to my story, all this took place in my mind. I think not."

He scratched his chin with his glasses. "You're right. When I spoke to the sheriff, Kenny Hobart, he believed Roy was missing, alright, but of his own volition. I told you, remember?" Harry replaced his glasses, then discarded his old cigar and lit a new one. "On the other hand, this is an election year. If this does turn out to be murder, and that Hobart character were to solve it, albeit with your help, that would clinch his re-election." Harry took several puffs and considered his next statement carefully. "It's not like you wear flowing robes and have long, black fingernails, Kate. Why . . . you are probably the most conservative looking woman I've met in a long time. In fact, if you weren't so damned pretty, you'd be boring."

"Excuse me?" I'm fond of traditional clothes; they are never really in style but never really out of style either. Besides, it's like wearing a uniform. Low mental maintenance.

"Don't be insulted, Kate. I meant that as a compliment."

Harry gulped his tea. "I was trying to say that you don't look like some nut case. And you are a junior partner in an old and respected public accounting firm. The sheriff would be a fool if he didn't take you seriously." Harry puffed like a freight train. "Anyway, what have we got to lose?"

Harry's logic often amazed me. He had nothing to lose. I was about to remind him that I, on the other hand, had quite a bit to lose when something hit my rear bumper.

We whipped around and saw a wizened, Union colonel gallantly astride a magnificent black stallion. They were a study in antitheses. The colonel's long hair and moustache reminded me of the angel hair my grandfather used as snow in his Christmas garden. The horse and rider cut quite a figure in that Civil War theater.

The colonel apologized in an unexpectedly bold voice. "Mighty sorry, Sir, for tapping your car. King's Ransom and I are still getting acquainted." The old gentleman confessed blithely, "And we're both a bit headstrong." The horse danced about as the colonel prepared to dismount. I walked around to them, held the stallion's bridle, and rubbed its neck. Ransom calmed down immediately. The old gentleman climbed down from his saddle slowly . . . painfully slowly.

"Much obliged, Ma'am." The colonel removed his hat and bowed. "Ransom likes you. Been around horseflesh a lot haven't you?"

"Yes, I have. I have been riding since I was six and have a horse of my own." At the thought of my beautiful Irish mare, Flute, I beamed.

The colonel removed his leather gloves, fastened them to his belt, then locked his arm in mine. He led both Ransom and me to the taller grass between my car and the oak. Harry followed without a syllable. The colonel released my arm and struck a self-confident pose while allowing his horse to nibble grass. My disapproving glance prompted his comment, "I know a horse shouldn't eat with a bit in his mouth, but I'll only let him have a snack." The colonel's eyes glinted impishly. He lifted his tresses from his neck as if to cool himself.

"My family bought me Ransom when my old horse, Appomattox, died. Matty'd been my trusted companion nearly 30 years. I bought him the year I started re-enacting." His face grew solemn. "I tell you, there's nothing worse than losing a pet. And that's what old Matty was to me. Why, animals are like members of your family." The colonel paused and fanned himself with his hat, "Hell, my pets are more like members of my family than some of my own relatives!"

Harry returned my quizzical look.

The colonel raised his thin arm and pointed his arthritic index finger into the crowd. "Look there at my grandson, Lee. Other than his bad temper, he is no more like me or my son than the man in the moon." The colonel obviously assumed we knew his grandson. "He thinks he's too good to do construction work like us. Lee never liked getting his hands dirty." The colonel stared at his own hands and shook his head. "My grandson always said he'd find a more refined way to make a living." The colonel grasped his scabbard. "Lee's dad and I thought he would eventually come to his senses and join our family's contracting business. That would have been the proper thing for him to do. But no. My grandson got a part-time job one winter at the ski resort and took up with that Roy Allnutt. Lee had little time for his working-class kin after Allnutt filled his head with uppity ideas. Hell, oh pardon me Ma'am, I was relieved when Allnutt loaned Lee the money to go off to college. I got tired of hearing him praise that Allnutt clan and bad mouth our family. I tell you, Lee's mom, rest her sweet soul, was heartsick over that boy."

He used what appeared to be all the strength he could muster to lift Ransom's head from the grass. He lovingly stroked his stallion's nose and continued. "Me . . . I said good riddance to the traitor. I didn't have anything to do with Lee for a good many years. But, when he asked for our family's support in his bid to join our 139th Pennsylvania Infantry unit, his dad agreed without hesitation." The old man's furrowed faced turned suddenly pensive. "I had a sneaking suspicion Lee's motive for joining was not to heal old family wounds. I thought they were more likely to either impress somebody or to justify his expensive weaponry collection. I knew, in my heart, he wouldn't be an active member of our unit. But, that was the first time in a long time Lee had reached out to his dad. It made my son so happy. What was I to do? I backed Lee's membership."

I remember thinking we had struck a gold mine of local gossip in this gentleman. He could surely tell us everything we would ever want or not want to know about Roy Allnutt. I stopped chewing my lip and tried to invent an excuse to keep him talking. I found the old colonel most enjoyable. He was a vibrant spirit.

I was about to question him about the Allnutt clan when Elliott Danforth swaggered towards us. To my surprise, Elliott wrapped his arm around the colonel's shoulders. That jerked the old gentleman, and threw him off balance. After the colonel righted himself, he cleared his throat and remarked sarcastically, "Well, speak of the devil. Let me introduce you fine people to my grandson, Lee Danforth."

While feigning a smile, Elliott corrected the colonel, "Elliott. You know I prefer to be called Elliott, grandfather."

My mind raced to conjure a reason why Harry and I were still there, but Elliott did not question us. He requested instead that his grandfather join him at the mock battlefield to review some specifics of an upcoming event. We said our goodbyes, and the old colonel and Ransom left with Elliott.

Harry commented as we watched them leave, "I can see where Elliott gets his charisma."

Harry and I certainly agreed on that.

Harry handed me the watered-down iced tea I had left on the hood of my Volvo. I was about to take a sip when a familiar voice from behind the oak added, "Yes, Elliott has his share of charisma. And he has learned to use it to his advantage." Mark, looking dauntingly handsome in his indigo corporal's uniform, stepped from behind the tree. No wonder women in those days fell passionately in love with soldiers.

Mark's dogs, Charlie and Snowball, were absent. I asked lightheartedly, "Where are your two buddies?"

"Charlie and Snowball?" Mark's tone matched his stern countenance. "I never let them out during re-enactments. I would be afraid they might bolt and run with all of this noise, especially the gunfire. I wouldn't want to chance their getting lost."

I felt dwarfed by Mark as he approached us. Tension enveloped our unlikely trio. Being a man of few words, Mark proceeded brusquely, "Why are you here?"

Harry replied unconvincingly, "We saw the sign for the re-enactment when we turned off of Route 16 yesterday. Kate has become interested in the Civil War recently, so we thought we'd return today to see the show."

Bad choice of words, I thought. Harry would have made a poor diplomat.

"Re-enactments are *not* shows!" Mark attacked. "They are held to educate people about the customs and philosophies of the 1860s. Not to entertain a bunch of mindless thrill-seekers." Mark's blazing eyes betrayed his suppressed rage.

I attempted to object, but Mark allowed me no time to speak. He folded his arms across his chest and peered down at us. "Do you consider me naive enough to swallow your lie? You came here today to pry into my family's affairs." His operatic voice thundered, "We don't want you here. Please leave." Mark spun on his boot heels and marched back toward the oak. Before he disappeared behind its trunk, Mark growled, "Do as I say, or you could be sorry."

Harry reached into his pocket. "What was that all about?"

I spun Harry around and pushed him toward my car before he had the chance to retrieve whatever he was after. I answered, "I don't know, but I have my suspicions. I think it's time to talk to the sheriff."

Chapter 6

Montaview was a quaint town comprised of antebellum homes resting along streets that emanated from the town square like spokes of a wheel from its hub. That day, those streets teemed with people and cars. Residents and shopkeepers wore Civil War costumes, and every shop and restaurant advertised "Re-Enactors Welcome".

A church bell pealed as Harry drove along Main Street searching for the sheriff's office. The ringing came from a half-timbered church boasting, from the sound of it, a fully operational belfry. A wooden sign masterfully carved with black, Gothic lettering hung above the church's arched entrance, and announced "THE BELFRY—Unique Works of Art".

"Harry, stop!" I pointed at the church. "That must be Rowena's art gallery." For some inexplicable reason I felt excited by the prospect of meeting Rowena. "Let's stop here first. I am certain we will be able to find the sheriff later."

Luckily, a van pulled out of a parking space not far from the church. Harry parked my car and got out without so much as a hint of an argument.

I pushed open The Belfry's thick wooden door and was struck by the gallery's decor. The exposed beams and egg-shell stucco walls looked original. The choir loft, dais, and ornately carved altar served as displays for the gallery's offerings. The afternoon sun streamed through ten foot tall stained glass windows and illuminated the delicate porcelain plates and bells for sale.

As we made our way toward the altar I commented to Harry, "Marjorie has many of these bell designs in her collection. Rowena must have made them for her."

A melodic female voice corrected me. "That is only partially true." A pair of celadon eyes peeped from behind the vestry door. I saw in them a kind of genuineness many of us lack. I knew without Harry's confirmation those eyes belonged to Rowena. She hurried to greet us.

She took my hand in hers as I was sure she did an old friend's. "I am Rowena Allnutt, proprietress of this humble establishment. I was listening so intently to my Uncle Victor ringing the bells, I didn't hear you enter."

I was elated to find both Rowena and the mysterious Victor in the same place. Harry's glance indicated I should contain my enthusiasm.

In keeping with the Civil War theme, Rowena wore a long, green gingham day dress which accentuated her Rubenesque curves. Her skein of auburn hair was drawn up and back from her face except for several coils which dotted her brow and hung at her temples. At the time of the Civil War, round faces were fashionable, and women wore their hair up and flat on top with curls at their cheeks to give that illusion. Rowena needed no curls to emphasize the roundness of her lovely face. A trickle of freckles added a tinge of color to the young women's alabaster complexion.

Rowena and her mother, Marjorie, were both short, and I suspected Marjorie would have had Rowena's build if she had eaten more and drunk less.

Rowena said, "I want to give credit where credit is due. My partner, Helen, makes the plates and bells. She is a true artisan—I merely paint." Rowena paused, then held up a dainty but pudgy finger for emphasis. "However, I do make all of the wooden plate frames and bell stands." Rowena's curls bounced as she tilted her head toward the belfry stairs. "My uncle taught my brother and me woodworking. He is a man of many talents. Her tone revealed more than familial pride. Rowena sighed, "Uncle Victor is like a father to us."

A look of recognition swept over Rowena s' face as she shook Harry's hand. "Please excuse me if I'm staring. This probably sounds silly because I haven't seen this person in years, but you look very much like a college chum of my dad's."

Harry shone with delight. "That's because I *am* a college chum of your dad's. I'm Harry . . ."

"Templeton!" Rowena reached up and threw her arms around Harry's neck.

Harry reacted like a department-store Santa Claus receiving an unexpected hug from a child. Rowena insisted we have herbal tea and chat so we withdrew to her apartment behind the vestry. I noticed the bells stopped ringing during the reminiscing.

I was anxious to meet Victor. Harry's description of him was nothing like Rowena's. What had been Victor's real motivation for returning home after years of estrangement from his family? I hoped to intuit the answer by being in his presence and listening to him speak. Better yet, I hoped to sense whether Victor played a part in Roy's disappearance. Rowena and Harry were so busy chatting, I doubted either noticed my gooseflesh.

Harry asked Rowena when she had decided to pursue a career in art. Her voice cracked when she intimated that shortly after her diabetes diagnosis, her doting dad, Roy, turned inexplicably cold toward her. Rowena admitted that to spite him she abandoned her plans to join the family business and gave her undivided attention to her first love, art. A man entered the room as Rowena jokingly asserted she inherited her artistic abilities from her Uncle Victor. Except for the auburn highlights in his wavy brown hair, he could have been the man in my dream.

Rowena rushed to his side, slid her arm through his, and smiled up at him. "This is my favorite uncle, Victor."

The man kissed her forehead and commented, "Should I be flattered, my dear? If my memory serves me, I am your only uncle." He subdued a chuckle.

Harry stood to make the introductions. "This is my niece, Katherine St. George." I remained seated while Victor shook my hand. I felt reservation in Victor's handshake.

Harry continued amicably, "You probably don't remember me, but I was your brother's college roommate, and the best man at his wedding."

Victor's scowl betrayed an embittered man. He composed himself and shook Harry's hand. Victor replied stoically, "I did not attend my brother's wedding."

Harry was a fool. He was supposed to interrogate Victor not irritate him. If looks could have killed, Harry would have been killed on the spot—and not only by me. Victor's eyes were searing.

Rowena remarked in an unmistakably defensive tone, "Uncle Victor moved to the West Coast many years ago to study art. Surely, he would not have been expected to leave his studies for something as trivial as a wedding."

I thought hers an odd comment considering she was engaged to be married.

Harry returned to his seat and fiddled with an unlit cigar while trying to think of some way to placate Victor. He eventually said, "Rowena and Mark think you are quite a talented craftsman. In fact, Mark praised your work just yesterday."

Strike two. Harry was now zero and two.

"Yesterday?" Rowena interrupted Harry as she placed her tea cup onto its saucer. I noticed the hand holding her saucer appeared taut. "Were you at the lodge yesterday?"

Harry recognized his mistake. "Yes, we were. Katherine

and I drove up to check out the Magic Mountain Golf Course. And, since we were so close, I suggested we visit your family." Harry looked at Rowena. She looked anxious. Harry added, "But, Marjorie wasn't feeling well so our visit was brief."

I knew Victor did not believe Harry's shabby story any more than Mark had.

"Strange," Victor remarked while studying Harry's body language. "Marjorie failed to mention your visit to me."

Rowena ran the fingers of her right hand around the rim of her cup. She kept her eyes lowered. "Uncle, dear, if mother was suffering from another of her headaches, she probably was still asleep when you left this morning."

Victor must have surmised where the conversation was leading. He looked at Harry, then me, and said, "So you know Roy has been away and . . . ."

I finished Victor's statement. "And no one has heard from Roy for approximately three weeks."

Rowena looked shocked. "What has mother been telling you?" When Rowena realized how her response must have sounded, she explained, "I mean, mother should not trouble anyone outside the family with such matters. Thank the dear Lord mother rarely sees guests." Rowena tried to resume a more casual air as she finished her tea. As an afterthought, Rowena added with a stilted laugh, "If anyone took mother seriously, her babbling could make the Allnutts the laughingstock of Montaview."

Harry took the offense. "Your mother was not the one who told us your father has been away. I phoned several weeks ago to confirm plans with Roy for our college reunion. During that conversation, *you*, Rowena, informed me Roy was gone."

Rowena raised her eyebrows and pressed her left hand to her heart. I waited for her to raise her right hand, but she did not. Rowena's sparkling engagement ring was difficult to miss. I assumed that ring had been Elliott's choice because I couldn't picture Rowena as ostentatious.

"You are absolutely right, Harry," Rowena gasped. She covered her tiny nose and mouth with her freckled hands. "I had forgotten we had that conversation." She stared blankly while she tried to recall the details of their discussion. "Please forgive me if I sounded a bit testy that day. Mother and I had been disagreeing about my wedding date. Unfortunately, you called in the midst of our debate." Either Rowena was truly sorry, or she should be in the theater.

Victor had not moved from his original position. He calmly brushed a nonexistent fleck from his beige and green striped polo shirt. "When Roy left, we assumed he had gone to his reunion. However, when a week passed and Roy failed to return, we thought he might have gone off on one of his," Victor faltered, "one of his trips." All eyes were cast firmly on Victor. "What I mean to say is . . ."

"Hello, is anyone there?" A female voice echoed from within the gallery.

Victor was the closest so he opened the door and responded in what I perceived to be a relieved tone. "Someone will be with you momentarily." Victor cast a sly smile toward Harry and me. "Please excuse us. Rowena and I must attend to customers." Victor held the door open and motioned for us to move into the gallery. Victor hurried to help the woman standing at the foot of the altar admiring a porcelain figurine.

Rowena walked us to The Belfry's entrance. As we left, she said, "Thank you both for coming." She smiled guilelessly, "When Daddy returns, please come back to visit."

Rowena stood in the entranceway and waved as we walked toward my car. I waved back as I whispered to Harry, "We may visit again before her Daddy returns." We reached my car, and Harry leaned his elbow against the top of the passenger door's frame. Naturally, he lit one of his vile cigars.

Harry puffed, deep in thought. I craned my neck looking up and down the street for the sheriff's office. "The more I see of the Allnutts, the more certain I am they are hiding something. I say we find the sheriff and tell him about the vision I had at the Allnutt pond." Harry continued puffing, and nodded in concurrence.

I stepped in the direction of The Belfry. Harry grabbed my shoulder, and said. "I think it would be wise to have the Allnutts think we left town." Harry pointed down the street, "Let's go in that direction first. If the sheriff's office is not there, we can sneak around some of the back streets to get to the other end of town."

We had no luck finding the office on Main Street. We, therefore, walked down West Street which appeared to wind around behind the shops. The streets were so busy I failed to see how either Rowena or Victor could have noticed us among the crowd. We found the sheriff's office halfway down West Street next to a barber shop whose sign was an old-time, glass cylinder with red, white, and blue stripes spiraling down its face.

Apparently, Montaview experienced little crime. The sheriff's office was the size of a walk-in closet and had no visible cells. The office, itself, was furnished with a typical government-issue metal desk and matching bilious green chair. A pitifully small pair of antlers hung on the wall behind the desk. Two brown government-issue metal chairs sat to the left of the desk. Grey metal file cabinets lined one wall. Various stuffed creatures—including but not limited to a once-playful grey squirrel clutching an acorn and a once-beautiful red fox with its bushy tail extended as if in flight—gazed glass-eyed from atop each cabinet.

The office appeared to be a museum dedicated to someone's high-tech assault on indigenous wildlife. I have always believed, to make hunting a fair test of prowess, the hunted and the hunter should be comparably armed.

And have, since childhood, relished the thought of rabbit hutches decorated with glass-eyed heads mounted above the carefully hung hands and feet of the hapless human hunters who lost.

A sports commentator's voice blared from a fifties, black plastic radio beside a rotating fan on a radiator. A man with his back to us rested in the desk chair. His blonde hair was shaved in the military style, and perspiration dripped onto the headrest. His impeccably pressed uniform jacket hung on a tarnished brass coat tree. His head was cocked to one side, and he appeared to be either engrossed in the game or asleep. I surmised he was the sheriff.

To get the man's attention, Harry tapped on the desk with his knuckles. In one fluid motion, the man swirled around, sprang from his seat, and drew the gun from the holster at his hip. He aimed directly at Harry.

I know little about guns, but that one looked like a serious weapon. Harry and I both raised our hands in submission as Harry blurted, "Whoa buddy, we only want to talk."

The officer made a rapid assessment and decided we were innocuous. He replaced his pistol in its holster. He cleared his throat and straightened his tie. "I don't like people sneaking up on me. I guess I spent too many years in the Corps." He jutted out his chin and squared his shoulders as he reached over and twisted the radio dial to OFF. "There. That's better. I didn't hear you come in." He signaled permission to lower our hands as he took his seat.

The officer's wiry frame lead me to believe he was an exercise fanatic. His heavily starched, white shirt had a military crispness. The oppressive heat in his office apparently caused him no discomfort. My guess was he had grown up in Montaview, joined the Marine Corps after high school, taken his twenty-year retirement, and returned home to become sheriff. I supposed compared to Parris Island, this weather was balmy.

The officer made a half-hearted attempt to smile as he looked us over. "I guess I'm just a little jumpy today with all these tourists around. I like it when it's nice and quiet." He stretched back and lifted his feet to the desk top. I could have applied my makeup by the gloss on his shoes. "Please have a seat . . . such as they are." Again, he almost managed a smile. "I'm Sheriff Kenny Hobart. What can I do for you?"

Probably feeling somewhat emasculated by the sheriff's initial aggression, Harry replied forcefully, "What you should be asking is what we can do for you."

Harry straightened himself in his chair and puffed out his chest. I expected him to begin beating on it like a male gorilla vying for attention. Instead, he rose, walked to the side of the sheriff's desk, and glared down at him. Harry had unwittingly assumed the alpha dog position; but, from the look on the sheriff's face, Harry's attempt at dominance had failed.

Harry changed tack, and swaggered around the tiny office like a commanding officer reviewing his troops. Without asking, he lit a cigar. Harry smoked as he introduced us, then described my part in finding the Lennoxville police dog. Harry emphasized my partnership in a large old-line Baltimore accounting firm and my family's longstanding position in the community. If I ever run for political office, I would certainly consider Harry for my campaign manager.

The ice was broken, and Sheriff Hobart treated us to numerous hunting tales starring his beloved hounds, Leatherneck and Sgt. Major. I recognized the sheriff as someone who clearly enjoyed his canine companions as he described his dogs' antics. They may have been his only family.

Harry attempted to steer the conversation back on course. "Ms. St. George and I really came to talk to you about Roy Allnutt."

Hobart looked disappointed. His overbearing expression returned, and he snapped the pencil he had been doodling with in half. "Roy Allnutt! Why would you want to talk about him?"

I could restrain myself no longer. "Because Roy Allnutt has been missing for approximately three weeks, and I have a feeling I know what happened to him." I approached the sheriff's desk and planted myself directly in front of him.

Sheriff Hobart appeared surprised.

After my disclaimer about not being crazy, I proceeded. Sheriff Hobart nodded as I described the visions I had experienced last night and this morning. Those recollections were still so disturbing I felt nauseated and light-headed. Harry must have noticed because he quickly moved a chair behind me and urged me to sit. He then moved his chair next to mine. He crushed his cigar in the ash tray on the sheriff's desk.

Sheriff Hobart offered me a cup of water from the water cooler. He allowed me to swallow several sips before he bent over me like a school yard bully. He folded his arms behind his back. The sheriff pushed his face toward mine until I could smell his Breathsavers. Sheriff Hobart pronounced each word distinctly, "What exactly do you expect me to do with your so-called visions, Ms. St. George?"

"I expect you to search for Roy Allnutt's body at the Allnutt's pond," I replied defensively. Then I shoved my chair away from the sheriff. "And . . . and . . . I expect you to interrogate the Allnutt family." I could feel my jaw becoming rigid. "If you ask me, they are all suspects in Roy's disappearance."

Hobart stood up, did one irritatingly slow lap around his office, then perched on the corner of his desk. His face reminded me of a weasel. "I think you are crazy as hell, lady," he asserted. To drive his point home, Sheriff Hobart then picked up his letter opener and jabbed it into his desk blotter.

Harry jumped up and thrust his fist at the sheriff's chin.

"Wait a damned minute there, Hobart," Harry retorted. "I won't allow you to speak to her that way!"

Harry never ceased to amaze me. Perhaps chivalry was not dead.

Sheriff Hobart grabbed Harry's shoulders and eased him back into his seat. "You two have got it all wrong. This Allnutt thing is nothing to get yourselves upset about. Talk has it that for the last nine or ten years, Roy Allnutt has been quite a womanizer." Hobart resumed his seat at his desk and removed his letter opener from the blotter. He fingered the opener as if savoring its rigidness. "There seems to be a lot of gossip about why Roy suddenly changed from a loving family man to a miserable lech—but that's what happened. Old Sheriff Tate told me right before he retired that one day Roy just started drinking and carrying on something terrible. And as far as I can see, Roy hasn't let up yet."

The sheriff got himself a drink from the cooler. "That stupid son-of-a-bitch picks up women at the golf club right next door to his place. I remember hearing one of Roy's women was from Baltimore. Her husband was a golf-crazy banker. That guy dragged his wife up here to the country club every weekend from March to November. She didn't play, so I guess she got bored."

Hobart gulped his water. "Word has it that Roy and that woman from Baltimore were playing house in her suite at the club while her husband was playing eighteen holes." The sheriff chuckled. He must have recognized the irony of his statement. "The banker must have come back from the course early one Saturday afternoon and caught the two of them because one of the bartenders told me there was quite a commotion and the banker stormed out of the club with his wife screaming after him."

The sheriff yawned. "From what I hear, though, Roy and his women usually leave Montaview altogether. Sometimes they are gone for days. But, like I tell the husbands when they complain to me, there's nothing I can do about it. I tell them, 'You got to keep your women in line. Show 'em who's boss.'"

I looked at the ceiling and thought. Thank you Sheriff Hobart for the Neanderthal approach to marital harmony. My curiosity got the best of me. "Does Roy's family know about his affairs?"

Hobart scratched his head, "I wouldn't exactly call them affairs. None of them last that long."

"Well, whatever you want to call them—peccadilloes, indiscretions?" I shook my head in disgust. "Does Roy's wife, Marjorie, know about them?"

The sheriff sighed, "Local gossips say she doesn't. Marjorie's brother-in-law, Victor, and her son, Mark, are very protective of her." Hobart hesitated a moment. Then, despite the fact that Sheriff Hobart, Harry, and I were the only ones present, the sheriff cupped his hands around his mouth and whispered, "Mrs. Allnutt has a drinking problem."

Harry added solemnly, "Considering Roy's philandering, perhaps that is a blessing. Often sadness forces a person to seek solace in a bottle."

Oddly, I felt like we had hit on an important fact. "But didn't you mention Roy was once a good husband? Did Marjorie's drinking drive him away?"

"Not that I know of," the sheriff replied. "I think she started drinking right after her daughter, Rowena, got real sick with diabetes." Hobart stood and stretched his legs. "Come to think of it, Sheriff Tate said that was around the time Roy started acting up. Strange how some things just happen."

Harry sounded impatient, "Let's return to Ms. St. George's suspicion that Roy has met with foul play."

Sheriff Hobart suddenly realized he had encountered Harry before. Hobart turned to Harry and sneered, "You're the newspaper guy who called here weeks ago and asked about Roy."

I found it difficult to believe it took the sheriff that long to recognize Harry's distinctive voice.

"Yes, I am." Harry persisted, "At that time, you insisted Roy would return home soon. Are you ready to admit you were wrong?"

"HELL NO!" Red splotches inched up Hobart's neck. "That ole devil will show up any day now. And I don't want the two of you hanging around town asking questions and bothering folks." The sheriff opened his office door and waved Harry and me out. "We don't need any help from outsiders. We take care of our own around here." When Harry and I reached the cobblestone street, Hobart yelled, "Anyway I'm a Christian. I don't believe in that psychic witchcraft bullshit."

The sheriff slammed his office door. I turned around and saw him peek at us through the Venetian blinds as we walked away.

Harry laughed, "I guess he's afraid you'll put a spell on him."

Sheriff Hobart's dig hurt even though I attempted to ignore it. "But, I am a Catholic, albeit a recovering one. What did I do to give him that impression?"

"Don't take that idiot's remark to heart. That's not like you, Kate." Harry patted my shoulder. "I noticed an attractive restaurant on Main Street. Since we haven't had anything to eat, let's stop in there and have a nice dinner."

"That sounds lovely, Harry. Thank you."

The Montaview Inn was an elegant stone mansion which had been converted to a combination bed and breakfast and restaurant. The vestibule and lobby were furnished with fine Federalist and Empire antiques. The Smoking Parlor off of the lobby was similarly appointed. The ecru ceiling had a dull overcast resulting from more than a century of cigarette, cigar, and pipe smokers.

The restaurant was comprised of several cozy rooms, each

with a formal fireplace which would be delightful in winter. The menu offered many gourmet and several vegetarian entrees. I reflected on the events of the last two days while perusing the menu. After the waiter took our order, I sipped my spring water with lemon and admitted, "Harry, perhaps I am making too much of my dreams and visions. Finding one police dog does not make me a psychic. Maybe I got caught up in your concern for Roy and I allowed my imagination to color my judgment."

Harry sniffed the cigar he rolled between in fingers. However, because of the "SMOKING ALLOWED IN THE PARLOR ONLY" sign in the lobby, his conscience prevented him from lighting it. Harry ogled the weed and said, "As much as I dislike Hobart's attitude, he may be right about Roy's history of womanizing. It sounds like everyone in town, except poor Marjorie, knows about Roy's shenanigans. And, I have to admit, Roy was quite a lady's man in college." Harry chuckled, "Roy had the women standing in line. Seemed like he could have had anyone he wanted. In fact, everyone was surprised when he returned from Easter break our senior year and announced he had met 'the girl of his dreams'. Every weekend after that, Roy drove back to Maryland to see her. Roy told me this girl—Marjorie—was enrolled at Hood College. All of Roy's buddies were shocked when he announced his intention to marry her as soon as he graduated that June." Harry swallowed his Coke thoughtfully. "Don't get me wrong, Kate, Marjorie was a real charmer. Actually, I recall Roy boasted he had stolen Marjorie from another admirer." Harry rubbed his chin, "but I don't remember Roy ever saying who that admirer was." Harry took another swallow, "After all this time, I guess that's not important."

The waiter brought our salads. I tasted my first bite and realized I was famished.

Harry reached across the table before beginning to eat, and tapped my plate with his fork. "I'm sorry I involved you in this wild goose chase. This whole thing has been a huge waste of your time and energy." Harry stared into my eyes. His tone was sincere. "I should have listened to you. Please forgive me, Kate."

Why is it, the moment you fill your mouth with food, someone invariably says something to which you are expected to reply? I chewed and swallowed quickly. "You are forgiven, Harry. Actually, it has been . . .," I searched for the right word and contorted my mouth to form something resembling a smile, "interesting." After tonight, I would finally get my wish. Harry Templeton would go away.

While we ate our salads, Harry and I engaged in the superficial conversation polite people resort to when they know relatively little about one another. After our entrees were served, I asked, "Harry, didn't you tell me you were married?" I cut into the delectable-smelling carrot and mushroom loaf. "Please, tell me about your wife and family."

Harry stared at his plate and pushed his food around with his fork. "I was married, but we are not together now."

I teased, "Poor Harry. Your wife divorced you. I can not imagine why."

Silence. As I ate, I prepared to aim another barb at Harry. However, when I looked up from my meal and into Harry's face, I refrained.

"No, Kate, she did not divorce me." Harry heaved a burdensome sigh, "She died."

My throat felt constricted. I was barely able to swallow my food. Now I felt like the fool. I stared at the satin drapes behind Harry. I wished I could disappear behind them.

I wanted to apologize but found it difficult. I put down my fork and patted my mouth with the linen napkin. I chewed the inside of my lip childishly.

"Don't be embarrassed, Kate. Yours was a perfectly reasonable question." Harry's words were meant to be comforting, but the sorrow in his eyes magnified my guilt.

I sipped my iced tea. Finally, I said, "I am so sorry, Harry. I did not mean to upset you." I sat my glass on the table and nervously rubbed the edge of the tablecloth between my fingers.

Harry put down his fork. "Really, Kate, you have nothing to be sorry for." He pushed his chair away from the table like a man who had lost his appetite. "I, on the other hand, have everything to be sorry for."

I sat rigidly in my chair. My stomach tightened. I did not want to hear the story Harry was about to tell me.

"My wife, Mary, was the most loving creature on God's green earth. When I was young, I was your typical journalist, you know, always on the trail of some hot story. Running here, there, and everywhere for a by–line. I was so focused on my career, I made no time for anything except work . . . not even women."

I felt like a priest in a confessional.

"Not that anyone was brokenhearted about that. I was not exactly in demand." Harry assessed himself, then shrugged his shoulders. "Anyway, one day I was racing across town to cover a story when a cat darted in front of my car. I slammed on my brakes, but I felt my right front wheel roll over the poor thing. I thought I was going to be sick." Harry grasped the front of his shirt. His voice became feverish. "I crawled under my car to see how badly the cat was hurt. I have to tell you, I expected the worst. Those damned idiots behind me kept honking while I pulled the cat out from under the car." Harry began to perspire, as if he were reliving that moment. "Blood gushed from his hind quarters. When I picked him up, I used my suit jacket as a stretcher to keep the little guy still. Then I laid him on the passenger seat and wrapped my jacket around him to prevent him from going into shock."

I could not help wondering why Harry was so knowledgeable about emergency treatment for animals. Harry must have read my mind. "As a kid, I had worked at a small vet clinic on Falls Road. So, I rushed the cat there."

As usual, Harry needed something to occupy his hands. He reached into his pocket and removed his cigar lighter. "I ran into the clinic and explained to the receptionist what had happened. She called for a technician, and they both followed me to my car. The receptionist petted the cat's head and spoke to him lovingly while the technician examined him. Then the technician lifted the cat very carefully and carried him into the clinic. I remember pacing beside my car. The receptionist took my hand and lead me into the waiting room. She sat next to me, and said, 'At least you stopped and tried to help. That's what really counts.'"

Harry intertwined his fingers as if in prayer. "From that moment on, I knew I wanted to spend the rest of my life with that woman." Harry anticipated my next question. "The vet said the cat's pelvis was broken and his right, hind leg was crushed. His leg needed to be amputated, and his pelvis required costly surgery. Since the cat was obviously a stray and probably had additional medical problems, the vet suggested euthanasia. I just told him, 'Absolutely not! If you are willing to try to save him, I'm willing to pay whatever it costs.'" Harry thumped his fist on the table.

A waiter walking by gave Harry a reproving look.

"Did the cat survive?"

"Sure did." Harry perked up a little. "I visited him daily. And Mary, the receptionist, and I became great friends." Harry looked at me and smiled. "We began dating; and by the time the little guy was well enough to be released, we were engaged. Mary named him Tripod." For some unknown reason, Harry found it necessary to explain, "You know—three legs. Get it, Kate?"

I nodded.

"Funny, after Tripod was cleaned up, he turned out to be

white. And, believe it or not, he was deaf. Many white cats are deaf. Did you know that, Kate?"

I thought if I could keep our conversation focused on Harry's cat, I could avoid hearing the remainder of his story. "Yes, I did. I found my white cat, Vivian, under a car on Paca Street one scorching August afternoon. She was so emaciated, she looked like a specter. Naturally, I rushed her to my vet. That's when my vet told me about white cats being prone to deafness. The vet tested Vivian and determined she was not. Even if she had been, I would have kept her."

Harry removed a photo from his wallet and placed it on the table in front of me. "This was our first Christmas together, Tripod, Mary, and me. Mary and I had just returned from our honeymoon in the Big Apple." Harry assumed a faraway stare. "Mary loved the theater. To surprise her, I pulled some strings and got tickets to every show on Broadway. It cost me a bundle, but Mary was ecstatic."

I looked at the photograph. Mary appeared to be a women in her mid-thirties. She wore her chestnut hair cut in a bob. She had a good-natured, intelligent face. Her eyebrows were dark and had probably never been tweezed. Her brown eyes were not made-up, but I saw no need. Mary's smile was subtle but genuine, and she wore a touch of lipstick. Harry and Mary were hugging each other and a scrawny white cat wearing a Santa Claus hat slouched over one eye. Mary looked to be about Harry's height. She wore a slim, traditional herringbone wool skirt and white blouse with a Peter Pan collar. Her only adornment was her plain gold wedding band. I was certain Mary's humble beauty mirrored her soul. She reminded me of my fourth grade teacher. She was my absolute favorite.

I attempted to stay on this tack by commenting, "All three of you looked very happy."

Harry interrupted, "We were extremely happy together— Mary, Tripod and me. She brought a sense of order to my haphazard life. Even though I had been making good money,

I had no savings to speak of. She budgeted our money; and within the year, we had a hefty down payment for a house. Just as we were about to buy a house in Rodgers Forge, the *New York Times* offered me their crime beat. Not much more money, but a lot of potential. Mary and Tripod agreed—so we moved to the Big Apple. We could only afford a small house in New Rochelle, and money was tight. But our lives could not have been better."

Our waiter noticed we were not eating and asked if anything was wrong. Harry assured him our meals were fine; we were merely engrossed in conversation. Harry motioned for me to eat. I turned my attention to my dinner, and I was relieved to see Harry do the same. We ate in silence, listening to the conversations at the tables around us. I hoped Harry would content himself with eavesdropping and forego his sad tale. Unfortunately, he continued.

"Mary's and my fifth anniversary was coming up, and she wanted to give me something special. Mary remembered my mentioning I had always wanted an antique pocket watch, but had been too cheap to buy myself one. Mary evidently searched all over New York. She came home one Saturday and announced she had found several reasonably priced watches in a pawnshop on the upper East Side. Mary wanted to buy me exactly what I wanted, so she asked me to go with her to select the one I liked best."

Harry swallowed his food. I noticed his hands tightening around his utensils. "Even though I thought the pawnshop's location was questionable, the following Saturday Mary insisted we look at the watches she had found." I heard the anger rumbling in Harry's voice as he spoke. "We weren't in that damned place ten minutes when two teenagers who were already inside the shop shouted, "Hey . . . hand over your wallets!"

As Harry's voice grew louder, other dinner conversations ceased. "We turned around to meet two punks with pistols aimed directly at us. The chicken shit shop owner ducked behind his counter. That rattled the kid guarding the door. He kept screaming, 'Don't move! You hear me?! Don't move!' The kid shifted his pistol from his right hand to his left. The other kid was only five feet from Mary and me. He yelled, 'G'me your money—just g'me your money!'"

Harry was practically shouting at this point. I could feel all eyes on us, but I did not care. Harry's hands were quivering. "I reached into my overcoat to give the punk my wallet when the sound of a gunshot filled the room. I felt a stinging, almost burning sensation in my back. I started to collapse. Mary lunged toward me trying to ease my fall. Suddenly, a second blast exploded behind her. The last thing I remembered was the tidal wave of Mary's blood rushing over me."

Harry wiped the trickle of tears from his cheeks with his napkin. We sat in silence. I could feel my maternal instincts surfacing. I was surprised because I rarely experience them with people. I could have been a mother tiger protecting her frail cub. At that moment, I would have pounced on anyone who approached our table. Our waiter was astute enough to stay away. I carried a miraculous homeopathic remedy, Calming Essence, with me for emergencies. I placed several drops of it into my water glass, then carried it to Harry's side. I bent down as if ministering to a troubled child, and handed Harry my water. I noticed his trembling hands were clammy as he took the glass from me. "Take several deep breaths, Harry, then drink some of this."

Harry did, then rested his elbows on the table and dropped his head into his hands. I waited while he composed himself. The other diners lost interest; the sound of muted chatter, and silverware pecking at food once again filled the room.

"Perhaps I should take you home," I offered quietly. "It is obvious how miserable this has made you."

Harry rubbed his temples. "No, Kate. If you don't mind,

I think it is good for me to talk. Keeping this bottled up has just fed my bitterness."

"That is fine, Harry, if you really think you are up to it."

Harry took another sip of my water. "Before I opened my eyes, the antiseptic odor warned me I was in a hospital. Mary's parents and her brother, Morgan, sat at my bedside. Grief draped the room like a pall. My heart knew the answer, but I had to ask the question. 'How is my Mary?'"

"Mary's mom began to cry as she hurried from my room. Mary's dad went after her. The somber lines of Morgan's face should have provided my answer. Morgan's inflamed eyes stared at the pillow behind my head as if I wasn't there. Then he got up and walked slowly toward the window. Morgan stood silently looking out."

"I couldn't stand it any longer. I had to know the truth. I struggled, but managed to prop myself up. I called his name, but he ignored me. Again, I asked, 'Where is my Mary?'"

"Morgan turned to me and answered, 'Harry, our Mary is dead. God help us. Mary is dead!'"

"After that, all I remembered was Morgan yelling, 'Nurse, come quickly. He's ripping out his IVs!'"

Harry wiped his hands on his napkin repeatedly as if that might wipe away his guilt. "The hospital social worker told me I was in denial for weeks. Morgan took Tripod back to Baltimore while I recuperated from my back wounds. When I was ready to be released, I hired a live-in housekeeper to help me out until I could manage on my own. I called Morgan as soon as I settled in to ask when he could bring Tripod home." The sadness reflected in Harry's face was as fresh as if this had happened yesterday. "Morgan said I had been careless with Mary, and I caused him to lose his sister. Since Tripod was Morgan's only living reminder of Mary, he would not give me the opportunity to be careless with Tripod too. As soon as I was able, I traveled to Baltimore to try to regain custody of Tripod. But Morgan wouldn't budge."

"So you never saw Tripod again?"

"Morgan sent me photos and kept me informed about him." Harry motioned for our waiter. "In retrospect, I realize Morgan didn't understand how much I needed Tripod. Morgan was blinded by his grief and could not see that Tripod was very much a part of Mary and me. I tell you, Kate, losing both of them . . ."

Our waiter stood at Harry's side with our check in hand. Harry paid in cash. Harry whispered to me as we left the dining room, "I hope I didn't embarrass you too much, Kate."

I put my arm through his and answered loudly enough for everyone to hear, "You did not embarrass me in the least, Harry."

I decided to drive home and let Harry relax. I put Enya's *Watermark* in the tape player and headed toward Route 15 South. As I drove I thought about the conversation we had had Friday evening at the Mount Washington Tavern. When Ric had recognized Harry as *The Sun's* crime reporter, Harry had mentioned working the crime beat for the *New York Times*. He then made some vague comment about things happening and fortunes changing. Now I understand what he meant.

Harry must have read my mind. He said, "Kate, I was not a drinker until after Mary died and Tripod was taken from me. I knew Morgan was right. My carelessness had killed Mary. The more I thought about it, the more I hated myself. I lived in my own private hell. I believed I had no real friends, and I talked to no one about my feelings. I began telling my troubles to a bottle. At first, I hoped booze would relieve my sorrow, but grief returned as soon as I sobered up. I could not stand the pain so I drank constantly. For the first few months, I don't remember my drinking affecting my work. Eventually, though, I missed meetings, deadlines, then work altogether. That continued for another year. My editor, a damned great guy named Robert Machin, finally fired me. Don't give me that look, Kate. After he fired me, Machin immediately managed to get me checked into Sheppard Pratt to get me the help I needed. Honestly, that was the best thing Machin or anyone else could have done."

"So that is why you returned to Baltimore."

"Right, Kate, my beauty. When I dried out, Machin wheedled me a job at *The Sun* writing obits." Harry chuckled and scrunched his face. "Well, I had to start some place. It has taken me years, but I have worked myself back into the crime beat. I am finally getting my life together, such as it is. And I am staying sober."

I tapped Harry on his knee, "It appears you are doing a fine job of it."

I looked to my right as I spoke, and noticed a wooden sign that read, "Cunningham Falls State Park". I pulled into the entrance.

"What are you doing?" Harry's voice sounded amused.

"This may sound crazy, but I have an inexplicable urge to drive through the park. Twilight is approaching, but there is still enough light. You will enjoy the falls; they are enchanting." I had no idea what made me say that. This was the first time I had been in this park.

Harry settled back into his seat, "Fine with me. Carry on, Jeeves."

I drove along the winding, blacktop road. The only sound in the car was the Enya tape. While I listened to her hauntingly beautiful music, something told me that when I reached a fork in the road, I should bear right. I tucked that away for future reference.

When I had driven for several minutes longer, the fork appeared. The sign in the middle of the grass plot read "Falls" with an arrow pointing left. However, my instincts had urged me to turn right, which is exactly what I did.

Harry bolted up and exclaimed while pointing back at

the sign, "Kate, you missed it. The falls were to the left."

My voice was that of a rebellious child, "I do not care about that sign, Harry. I am going in this direction."

Harry snuggled back into his seat. "Okay, my beauty. Go where ever your heart desires. I am just along for the ride."

I wound through the park at a leisurely pace. I had the strange feeling I was looking for something but I had no idea what. I came upon a road marked "State Vehicles Only". Having no idea why, I proceeded down the forbidden road. Harry did not say a word. The blacktop ended but a dirt road continued deeper into the woods. I left the blacktop and followed the dirt road. I felt Harry's wide-eyed stare.

"Kate, are you crazy?" Harry's head bobbed up and down as he held onto the handle of the glove box. "Do you want some park ranger to lock us up?"

"Don't be such an old poop, Harry. Where is your sense of adventure?" I hoped my old Volvo's suspension could handle the road.

I ran over a huge bump, and we both hit our heads on the ceiling. Harry was in the midst of some profanity, when he stopped abruptly. "Look over there!" Harry squashed his chubby index finger against the passenger window. His words were those of an impatient, inquisitive child.

I stopped the car, and we jumped out to investigate. From the damage to the tree trunks and bushes, something had clearly ripped a path through the woods. The evening sun set the woods aglow as we followed what appeared to be tire tracks. But for us, the forest seemed abandoned. The only sounds were the crackle of the twigs beneath our feet. About twenty-five feet ahead a mound of debris—dead branches and underbrush—laid in our path. As we moved closer, I saw a long, low, metallic object gleaming underneath.

Before I could venture a guess, Harry shouted, "My God, Kate. That looks like Roy Allnutt's Jaguar!"

Chapter 7

The next morning, I entered my outer office to find my secretary, Suzy, wearing a tight, burnt umber, silk dress which was barely distinguishable from her tanned skin. She resembled a sea cow sporting a blonde wig. I said, "Good morning, Suzy. Did you have a pleasant weekend at the beach?"

Reaching into a three-quarters empty bag of caramel rice cakes, Suzy licked her sticky lips before she answered, "It was just too hot and humid . . . even for me. I had to eat ice cream and drink Diet Pepsi all day so I could sunbathe on that sweltering beach." Suzy pressed her can of Slim-Fast against her broad cheek as if she were still suffering from the heat, and continued in her nasal whine, "The cleaning people must have moved my candy dish, and now I can't find it."

I assumed Harry had done the deed Friday evening during our initial meeting, but I was not about to open that can of worms.

"I've just had one of my morning snack attacks," Suzy pouted, "and I had to eat most of these nasty old things." Suzy removed a rice cake from its bag and examined it briefly. Then she devoured it with quick, snapping bites like a ravenous Brobdingnagian gobbling some unfortunate creature. With each bite, the breaking rice cake crackled like bones splintering under the force of her jaws.

I clenched my teeth.

Despite her physical abundance, Suzy had tiny, almost stunted, fingers. She wiped her mouth as daintily as she could with a floral paper napkin she grabbed from the bottom drawer of her desk. Suzy's social-climbing mother would have been proud of her daughter's attempt at grace. "You know, Katherine, you have to eat a lot of rice crackers to feel satisfied."

"I suppose *you* do, Suzy." I escaped into the sanctity of my office. After laying my briefcase on the floor next to my desk, I sat down wearily in my desk chair. I wondered what happened to the diet Suzy was trying last week . . . or the diet she tried the week before . . . or the diet she tried the week before that. I suspected Suzy was one of those unlucky people who found both joy and solace in food. No matter what her mood, she found a reason to eat.

I rested my elbows on my desk top and held my head in my hands. I hoped the coolness of my fingers rubbing my temples might help to calm my racing mind. Last night my dreams were filled with bells pealing, saws buzzing and rifles firing. In one dream I vividly envisioned myself being shot by someone wearing an indigo uniform. Perhaps this Halloween, I should avoid masquerade parties.

I lifted the top piece of correspondence from the pile in the middle of my desk. Before completing the first paragraph, my mind wandered to the events that had occurred the previous evening in Cunningham Falls State Park.

Unfortunately, I needed to read all of my correspondence this morning because the majority of my work week consisted of back-to-back meetings. I decided a cup of tea was exactly what I needed to keep my mind focused on business. I selected from my collection a mug decorated with a beige cat watching fish swim in a small pond and walked into my outer office where the tea pot simmered on the hot pad. Suzy stood at the window and complained to herself about her new dress shrinking mysteriously before she had worn it while I made my tea and carried the steeping mug back into my office unnoticed.

I sat down and sipped my chamomile tea. I picked up that first letter addressed to Ms. Katherine St. George, Managing Partner . . . Much as I tried to dismiss it, the scene at Cunningham Falls State Park filled my mind. I attempted to convince myself nonbusiness topics were best kept out of the office. Since that was part of the sermon we asked our office manager to preach each time a new administrative employee was hired, the same should apply to a partner.

I swirled my chair around and peered out of the window behind my desk. Despite my resolve, my thoughts returned to the events of last evening.

I allowed myself to return to the shadows of the park. After finding the Jaguar, Harry had called Sheriff Hobart from my cell phone. I recall at the time thinking it strange that Harry remembered the number. He explained the phenomenon by admitting he had committed the number to memory the first time he had rung the sheriff. Harry had joked, "It was easy—the number was (717) SHERIFF." Some of Harry's quirks were amusing.

Harry and I had snooped around the Jaguar shamelessly while waiting for Sheriff Hobart to arrive. Harry warned, "Don't touch the car or any of its contents without gloves. We don't want Hobart finding our fingerprints all over this thing or he will swear we planted it here."

"It is summer, you fool. Why would I be carrying gloves?"

"Oh, sorry, Kate. I forgot." An aura of genius lit Harry's jovial face. He offered me a paper tissue, but I declined, "I have my own, thank you." I removed my Irish linen handkerchief from my pants pocket. I should have thought of that first.

"That's good. I can use this one myself," Harry observed as he wrapped the tissue around his right hand.

While Harry tried to examine the car's exterior, I was more intrigued by the Jag's interior.

The top was down; and despite the brambles and dirt, I determined the car had been impeccably kept. I pushed aside some branches to get a better look.

Harry scolded, "Don't move anything!" I jumped back and chewed the inside of my lip. I felt for a moment as if I were three years old again, and standing in my parent's living room where mother loomed between me and the Lenox figurines on her tea table.

Harry continued, "Cops get pissed when their evidence is tampered with." I wondered what my mother's excuse had been.

I circled the car, craning my neck, trying to see through the debris. I thought I saw a buff-colored business card lodged between the driver's seat and the carpet, but the impinging darkness distorted everything. I was about to crawl inside the car to have a closer look when I spied lights coming down the path.

Harry was preoccupied under the Jag's front end. I wondered how he could see anything without a flashlight. Knowing I had little time, I eased my arm through the branches and snatched the card. I slipped it into my pants pocket and turned to face Sheriff Hobart's warm greeting. "How the hell did *you* find this car?"

I explained what had happened, then asked the inevitable question, "Is this Roy Allnutt's Jaguar?"

Sheriff Hobart ignored me as he swaggered around the camouflaged automobile. Hobart beckoned for his deputies. They pushed Harry and me out of their way as they ran to Hobart's side. The sheriff barked commands, and his deputies leapt to follow them. Sheriff Kenny Hobart was in his glory.

Neither Hobart nor his men glanced in Harry's or my direction. After about a half hour, Harry tired of waiting and approached Hobart, who was now standing on the sidelines watching his men perform like trained seals. Unfortunately for me, Harry and the sheriff were out of ear shot. Harry's and Sheriff Hobart's facial expressions and their posturing had all the earmarks of an argument. Everyone stopped and watched as the encounter escalated. Harry suddenly was nose to nose—or more accurately—belly to belt buckle with Hobart. Harry pummeled the sheriff's shoulders with his open palms. The sheriff lost his balance and fell backward over a stump. Even the twilight could not hide the crimson cast to Sheriff Hobart's face. He catapulted up, his body heaving like an enraged bull. He charged Harry, thrust himself into Harry's mid-section, then slung Harry over his shoulder like a sack of meal. That was no mean feat for so slight a man.

The sheriff carted Harry toward me and dropped him at my feet with a *thud.* I crouched next to Harry while he gasped for air. Sheriff Hobart's shoulder in Harry's stomach must have knocked the wind out of him. Harry eventually caught his breath, then demanded, "We are getting the hell out of here!"

I helped him up and asked while I brushed the dirt from his pants. "Harry, what did Sheriff Hobart say?"

"Not now," Harry growled through clenched teeth. Harry staggered, hunched over, and held his stomach. "Hobart wants us out of here so we are definitely leaving. Got it?"

I wrapped my arm around Harry's waist as far as it would reach and led him down the path. As we approached my car, a four-wheel drive skidded to a halt directly across the dirt road from us. I heard the vehicle's doors slam as I helped Harry into the passenger seat. I looked up to catch a glimpse of Victor, Mark, and Elliott running into the woods.

On our trek back to Baltimore, I gave Harry what I considered ample time to recover before plying him with questions. Harry however offered no answers, and his glower clued me he was in no mood to talk. I was disappointed but undeterred. I used our quiet time to conjure multiple scenarios as to why and how Roy's Jaguar came to be abandoned in Cunningham Falls State Park. I allowed each scenario to play out in my mind as if I were editing movie footage. Each scenario had only one thing in common. Each was punctuated by the same vision of a steep-pitched metal roof atop a large structure. I was unable to focus on the structure, only its roof. Perhaps it was a house. Perhaps a barn or a church. Perhaps I was seeing The Belfry.

When I pulled into the Railroad Museum's parking lot an hour later, Harry finally spoke. "Look, Kate, that nut case Hobart insists he does not want or need our help. He said if—and the operative word here is 'if'—that Jaguar turns out to be Roy's, it only means Roy or somebody dumped the car. Nothing more."

I parked next to Harry's MGB. I began to object when Harry's words stopped me.

"Sheriff Hobart made it abundantly clear he doesn't give a damn what you or I think, Kate." Harry grabbed my chin and forced me to look him in the eyes. I was taken back by his steeled determination. "Kenny Hobart said he'll handle this. He also said if we didn't butt out of his business, we'd be sorry. I've been counting, Kate, and we've been warned twice today. I think it's time we both bloody well listened!"

The buzz of the intercom brought me back to my office. Suzy said, "Sorry to interrupt, Katherine. But, I was wondering if you had any notes you wanted me to type for your meeting at noon."

"No." I paused. "No, thank you." I wondered how long I had been daydreaming. Had Suzy turned the air conditioning up again? She often complained that she was too hot. I could not understand why if Suzy did not like heat, she baked ritualistically in the sun on the Ocean City beach.

I checked the thermostat. It was set at the normal temperature. I wondered why I was so cold. I surveyed my office. Its formality comforted me. Every item in my office was placed precisely where I wanted it. Nothing was ever moved unless I moved it myself. Our cleaning crew had been given strict orders about that. I knew the exact position of every book, every note pad, every pencil. At home with my furry companions I am totally different.

I rose and walked across my office to the side window. I watched the squirrels romp on the lawn outside corporate headquarters and admitted the investigation of Roy Allnutt's disappearance was out of my control. I dislike it intensely when I am not in control. My stomach tightened. I chewed the inside of my lip.

I forced myself to return to the correspondence I attempted to read earlier. I needed to get some work done before my meeting. However, business seemed bland compared to my adventures of the past few days. I reminded myself I had something special to be thankful for other than, of course, my motley crew. I was finally rid of Harry Templeton. I felt relieved.

For the remainder of Monday, and all day Tuesday, Wednesday and Thursday, I could not shake the feeling Sheriff Kenny Hobart would eventually need Harry's and my help. Whether the sheriff would request our help was another subject.

Thursday evening around 7:30, Ric and I were about to leave my house for dinner. Early in the week Ric had phoned to plan our strategy for our weekend tennis match. I gave Ric a brief synopsis of Harry's and my excursion to Magic Mountain Ski Resort. However, Ric had been hungry for more details about my—as he referred to it—case. Ric offered to take me to dinner if I agreed to reveal every sordid detail. Although I refrained from admitting the fact to Ric, I had missed our time together the past two weekends. I accepted happily.

In the living room, Ric tried to brush my cats' and dogs'

hair from his navy cotton twills—the price he paid for rough-housing with them. I went into the kitchen to get my keys when the doorbell rang. The bell had rung a second time by the time I reached the front door. I opened the door to find Harry Templeton standing on my porch. My surprise must have been evident because Harry said apologetically, "Kate, I know you thought you were finally rid of me," Harry's voice and face exuded excitement, "but I have two pieces of info I think will interest you."

I stood to the side and gestured, "By all means, Harry, come in. You remember Ric Whitby, don't you?"

Harry grabbed Ric's hand, "Of course I do. How are you, my boy?"

"Very well, thank you, Harry. How about you?" Ric's warm smile hinted he, too, was fond of Harry. I realized what I had just thought and bit my lip.

"Fine, thank you." Harry glanced around and realized we were on our way out. He blushed and shuffled about nervously. "I see I've come at a bad time. Don't let me keep you."

Rather than tease Harry, I glanced quickly at Ric. He nodded in agreement. I offered, "We are going out to dinner. Would you like to join us?"

Without hesitation, Harry answered, "Great!"

At Ellicott City's Cacao Lane Restaurant, Ric requested a table on the roof top. In summer, the roof was transformed into an enchanting garden complete with fountain, plants, and potted trees. The tallest trees were decorated with tiny white lights. I felt like a miniature doll in a Christmas garden. The day's heat and humidity were dissipating, but remained a reminder Christmas was months away. I welcomed the coolness of the wrought iron chairs against my legs.

Before our waitress brought our menus, Harry announced, "I adopted a cat." My wide-eyes and gaping mouth did not deter him. "All that talk about Tripod last Sunday

made me realize how much I needed a companion animal."
He peered at me over his glasses. "Isn't that the politically
correct term for pet?"

Ric cackled as Harry continued. "My life is finally stable,
and I am sure I can be a responsible pet owner."

I thought about Harry's pitiful MGB. Harry must have
read my mind because he stated, "I cleaned my apartment
thoroughly, bought dye and preservative-free cat food, ce-
ramic cat bowls, litter and box, and toys before I went to the
animal shelter." Harry glanced at me out of the corner of his
eye. I caught Ric winking at him. "I decided I should adopt a
cat that was sure to be euthanized. You know, an ugly, old, or
sick one."

I knew too well about those types—all of mine were
rejects.

Harry rambled on, "I told the receptionist at the shelter
just that. She said she had the perfect cat for me. He had
been brought in that morning by some idiot who said he,
'couldn't take care of his cat anymore.' From the looks of the
poor thing, that son-of-a-you-know-what had *never* taken care
of his cat." Harry proudly whipped out a Polaroid of his cat
and handed it to me.

"Meet Hathaway." Harry offered seriously, "Cyclops was
the first name that came to mind, but I thought it might give
him a complex."

Ric clasped his hand over his mouth to contain his
laughter.

"I know he looks a little rough," Harry asserted. "But,
with good food, veterinary care, and lots of love, I am certain
Hathaway will be magnificent."

Ric and I stared at the photo. Harry was a true optimist.
The cat was emaciated, had no hair on its back legs, and only
tufts along its back. It was next to impossible to be certain,
but Hathaway appeared to be a short-haired tiger. His tail
had obviously been broken, and his face was scarred. If that

were not enough, Hathaway had only one golden eye. I thought the name Cyclops would have been a better choice.

Harry was a good soul to take on such a responsibility. I tried to hide my welling tears by dabbing my eyes with my handkerchief. "My allergies always flare up this time of year."

"Whatever you say, Katherine." Ric knew me too well. He spoke for both of us. "What a wonderful thing for you to do, Harry. Hathaway is very lucky to have found you."

Harry became pensive. "To the contrary, my boy. I was lucky to have found him." Harry rubbed his chin. "Hathaway looks like he ran afoul of some whacko S.O.B with a stick or something." Harry added, "Humans can be so damned cruel!" He paused to ponder that thought and took out a cigar. He lit it and puffed. "Don't worry, Kate, I don't smoke these things around Hathaway. I wouldn't want him to get cancer. The woman at the shelter said Hathaway was in such bad shape they would not waste their time offering him for adoption. I was furious that they wouldn't give him a chance. So I completed the application and paid for him right then and there. The receptionist advised me they would have to process my application. I couldn't adopt him until the next day." Harry's face registered the disappointment he must have felt. "I wanted to make sure Hathaway would be safe there . . . you know. I told them they better damn well not make a mistake and euthanize him because they thought I wasn't serious about adopting him. The woman assured me the cat would be waiting for me when I returned."

"I take it he was?" Ric asked as our waitress approached.

Harry positively beamed. He ignored our waitress and continued, "Not only was the cat there, but the shelter workers had bathed him and put a blue ribbon around his neck. I took Hathaway to the vet's immediately to have him checked out." Harry's voice sounded relieved. "Other than worms and malnutrition, he was okay." Harry directed his comments to me as if he had anticipated my line of questioning. "Hathaway was dewormed before we left the vet's office. And, I have been giving him vitamins, and nothing but top-quality food. When Hathaway is strong enough, I will have him neutered." Harry punctuated his sentence with a nod.

"Bravo, Harry!," I applauded. "You are aware, of course, that the only way to curb overpopulation is to have pets spayed and neutered." I knew I was proselytizing, but I did not care. Perhaps someone sitting at another table also got my message.

Ric reached across the table, his blue eyes teasing, and took my hand as if to calm any insult I might perceive. He warned, "Don't get Katherine on that subject, Harry, or we will never get to your other news."

Our waitress still stood beside our table, tapping her pencil on her pad, waiting to take our order. Ric apologized. We made our selections hurriedly, and she stomped off. I made a mental note to reduce her tip. Petulance has its price.

I returned to Ric's allegation with my right eyebrow raised in feigned irritation. "Wait a minute, Ric. You are just as much an animal advocate as I am."

Ric pinched my cheek, "Lighten up, Katherine, I was only joking. Tell us your other bit of news, Harry."

Harry leaned back in his chair and locked his fingers behind his head. Self-satisfaction filled his voice. Harry drew out each syllable as he continued to attack our lungs with the smoke from the stump he clenched in his teeth. "Guess who called me today at *The Sun*." Harry pretended to admire his chewed fingernails and buff them on his rumpled, button-down shirt.

My curiosity piqued, "I don't have a clue, Harry. Who?"

Harry stretched across the table and whispered, "Sheriff Kenny Hobart. That's who."

My large eyes widened until I was certain I resembled an owl. "Tell us about it," I begged. I felt like I was back in

Brownies; and we were divulging our deepest, darkest secrets—such as they were when we were seven.

"Well, at this point, there really isn't much to tell." Harry practically emptied his Coke in one gulp. "Hobart called this afternoon to inform me they ran the tag numbers and identified the Jaguar we found." Harry stopped and took one last puff from his cigar.

I squinted to register my displeasure at Harry's stalling.

Harry leisurely squashed the cigar butt in the ash tray and announced. "The Jaguar we found is Roy's." Harry reached inside his shirt pocket for another cigar. I wanted to grab his hand and say, "Enough with these silly weeds, get on with it!" but I refrained. Harry lit his cigar.

I attempted to soften my tone. "A-n-d . . ." I wanted to reach in and pluck the words from Harry's throat. He really brought out the worst in me.

"Don't be so impatient, Kate my beauty." Harry inhaled slowly, obviously enjoying every foul-smelling puff. "I'm getting to the best part."

I remarked, "I hope that will be sometime in my lifetime."

Harry opened his mouth to speak at the exact moment our waitress arrived with our dinners. Her penchant for poor timing was irritating. Ric and I abstained from eating while we waited for Harry to continue his story.

Instead Harry balanced his cigar on the table's edge and savored our undivided attention as he took several bites of his broccoli melange.

My hands clenched my utensils. "HARRY!" I demanded.

"Okay, Kate, okay." Harry swallowed, then wiped his mouth. "Hobart said that after we found Roy's car, the Allnutts were so upset, they immediately asked the local television station—I think he said it was WGTY in Gettysburg—"

"Who cares, Harry," I prompted, "get on with it." I threw

my hands up in desperation. Ric and I began eating our dinners.

Harry took another bite. "Anyway, the Allnutts made a plea on television for Roy to come home."

"They still believe Roy is missing?" Ric asked in an incredulous tone.

"Evidently. Even though Sheriff Hobart had already told the family about Kate's visions." Harry's voice sounded equally skeptical.

"Wait a minute, Harry." I laid my fork on my plate. "Are you telling us that Sheriff Hobart told the Allnutts everything I told him?"

"That's exactly what I'm telling you."

Ric frowned, "Sounds like they either didn't believe Kate . . ."

I completed Ric's comment, "Or for some reason, they wanted everyone to believe Roy was missing."

Harry stopped eating. He took a deep, thoughtful breath and exhaled slowly. "I don't think that was their intention." Harry looked to me for acceptance. "Sheriff Hobart said this afternoon, the Allnutts had specifically requested he enlist Kate's and my help with the investigation."

"But I thought Hobart . . .," I forgot my manners.

"Please, Kate, let me finish." Harry shook his finger at me like a teacher correcting an impertinent child. "The sheriff said that early this morning Mark's two dogs had brought home a long, thin, object covered with mud. From the composition of the mud, they determined the dogs must have unearthed it near the Allnutt pond. Hobart and his men searched the pond's perimeter, and found what Hobart described as something resembling a freshly-dug grave."

I laid my knife and fork on my plate and swallowed my last bite of food with difficulty. I raised my fingers to shield my eyes from what I knew I was about to see. My palms began to sweat. I chewed the inside of my lip as I mustered enough courage to ask, "What had Mark's dogs found?" A picture instantly invaded my mind. The object was a mud-covered walking stick with a brass Jaguar handle. And it was identical to the one the older man had carried in my dream.

Chapter 8

For the first time in my professional career, I was anxious for my work week to end. If Friday had not been filled with meetings and Suzy would not have whined about having to reschedule them, I would have taken a vacation day and returned to Montaview immediately. To my astonishment, I found the idea of participating in a real investigation thrilling. I held a perverse fascination for the prospect considering before now I had only vicarious exposure to crime through novels and movies. I convinced myself that even if I was totally wrong, and Roy had merely run off with a woman, my mettle would be tested. That, in itself, was invigorating.

Susan and Marcia were delighted to exercise Flute on Saturday. Ric was such a dear, he not only found my substitute for our tennis match, but offered to drop by later in the afternoon to feed my motley crew. Ric loved them almost as much as I did.

Early Saturday morning Harry and I headed for Montaview. Sheriff Hobart had asked us to meet him at the Allnutts' home before the participants arrived for another Civil War Re-enactment. As we passed through Emmitsburg, I distinctly heard church bells peal. Wanting to get his reaction, I asked, "Don't you think it is an odd time for churches to be ringing their bells, Harry?"

"I didn't hear any bells." Harry cleared his throat, then added, "Maybe you just thought you heard bells because you are nervous. I know I'm a bit edgy myself." Harry shook from head to toe like a dog after a bath.

I parked my station wagon at the main house, and Rowena, Mark, Marjorie, and Elliott came down the stone walkway towards us. Victor emerged from a converted summer kitchen beyond the main house and, after much dawdling, eventually joined the rest of the family. Sheriff Hobart waited for us at the walkway's end. His scowl exaggerated his angular face and suspicious eyes.

As soon as Harry and I got out of my car, Hobart rushed at us like a fox defending its lair. With his usual grace, Sheriff Hobart spat every word, "Lee . . ., I mean Elliott, said the family thought you two might be willing to help look into Roy's disappearance." The sheriff turned his ire to Harry. "Seeing as how you were his college friend and all."

We walked toward the house. The garden statuary looked more congenial than our hosts. Silence pervaded the garden like a rose blight. Evidently, no one felt comfortable approaching Harry and me. I felt like a teenager at her first dance. In time, Elliott left Rowena's side and brushed past Sheriff Hobart. His gait and puckered grin proved Elliott intended to greet us with his normal panache despite the prevailing awkwardness. Elliott grabbed my hand and held it in both of his. Elliott's hands sizzled.

"We . . . the Allnutts and me . . . want to thank you for taking time out of your busy schedules to come all the way from Baltimore to help us."

Harry looked beyond Elliott. He had probably noticed Marjorie's quivering chin. Harry stepped toward her, his arms outstretched. The silence broken, Marjorie must have felt free to head for Harry's sympathetic arms. Mark followed her protectively. In Harry's embrace, Marjorie burst into tears, sobbing uncontrollably on Harry's shoulder. Marjorie had captured everyone's attention so I slid my hand from Elliott's grasp and walked away. I could not help picturing Elliott in the court of Henry VIII dressed in gartered stockings and a plumed hat. He could have fared well during those tenuous times.

Victor had his arm around Rowena's shoulder and rested his cheek atop her head. I was not certain whether Rowena's doleful expression reflected her concern for her missing father or her concern for herself. In my opinion, being romantically involved with Elliott could test a woman's self-confidence. Rowena, however, did not seem to be the type of woman who wanted or needed the spotlight.

I walked away from the garden, and Elliott followed me like a bloodhound. I registered my displeasure with Elliott's unnatural closeness by stopping abruptly, twirling around, and stepping to the side to avoid being bulldozed.

Elliott recognized the reason for my maneuver, and sought to hide his embarrassment. "What would you like to do first, Katherine? I'm at your beck and call."

What I would really have liked was some space. I chewed my lip. I knew that comment would only serve to alienate Elliott and I might need him at some point. I answered instead, "I would like to see Roy's walking stick."

Elliott called over his shoulder, "Rowena, honey, would you bring Roy's walking stick to us?"

I did not recall offering Elliott a position on my team. While we waited for Rowena, Elliott bragged about his graduation from Dickinson Law School and his meteoric rise to partner in the prestigious law firm of Billings & Newkirk, P.A. I remembered with self-deprecation a time when I would have found Elliott's personality appealing. My ex-husband, Colin, would assuredly have found Elliott a kindred spirit.

Rowena approached us tentatively. Her face was damp with tears. She cradled her dad's walking stick in her arms until Elliott took it from her. He dangled the dirty stick from his finger tips a full arm's length from his immaculate chinos and polo shirt. Rowena frowned, uttered something inaudible, then retreated.

Harry shifted Marjorie to Mark's capable arms, patted Mark on his back, then joined Elliott and me. Harry took the stick from Elliott who relinquished it willingly. Harry examined the stick.

"I thought Sheriff Hobart said Roy's walking stick was covered with mud?" Harry asked.

Uninvited, Hobart joined our clique. "It was. And I told you not to clean it." His cunning eyes peered at Elliott. "Didn't I tell you that mud might be relevant? Damn it, Lee. I knew I shouldn't have left it with you."

Elliott reclaimed the stick. He appeared unruffled, "I did not clean it completely. Marjorie complained about bringing dirt into her house, so I did not think it would hurt to wash the filthy thing a little."

I was in no mood for bickering. I glared at Elliott and his navy eyes held mine. I held out my hand and, with my jaw taut, demanded, "Elliott . . . give me Roy's walking stick . . . now."

Elliott handed me the stick with a retaliatory slap across my open palm. I did not flinch. Refusing to give Elliott the satisfaction, I held my stare. Elliott surrendered finally, and looked away. I stepped toward the pond; Elliott stepped in the same direction. I swung my open hand at his chest as a warning for him to stay back. "I want Harry to accompany me. Only Harry."

I was beginning to feel Harry and I were a team. Harry appeared pleased as my portly partner raced, so to speak, to catch up with me. I asked as we walked along together, "When we get to pond, would you keep an eye on the Allnutts?"

"Sure, Kate." Harry paused a moment. "Oh, I get it." His jovial tone sounded suddenly shrewd. "You want me to take note of their reactions while you do whatever it is you do."

"Precisely."

I stood on the spot where, last Sunday, I experienced being sucked into a quagmire. I ran my fingers over every inch of Roy's walking stick. The more I felt the particles of dirt and the smooth ebony beneath, the more that same queasiness gripped me. The muscles in my abdomen tensed. I felt an inexplicable urge to flee. I inhaled deeply, reminding myself I had committed to helping the Allnutts, and am loath to breaking commitments. Of course, I was certain Colin would have disagreed. In the heat of the only argument we ever had, after I had told him I wanted a separation, he accused me of abandoning my commitment to him. Colin had been right.

I stood at the edge of the Allnutt's pond, and at that moment I knew I needed to remain calm and focus solely on Roy Allnutt's walking stick. I exhaled slowly and thought, "God help me to see what happened here."

I tried to suppress my apprehension by taking several more deep breaths. The scent of Harry's cigar reassured me. I closed my eyes and focused on my words, "I have nothing to fear. I have nothing to fear."

I forced myself to become the man that I had previously envisioned being shoved into the shallow pit. As that man lay in the pit on his back unable to move, I felt the damp crust of dirt beneath his palms. I felt his heart beat faintly as the excruciating pain in the middle of his forehead faded into numbness. I felt his hands and feet cooling as his waning heart pumped sporadically. I sensed the weight of the dirt pelting his limp body burdened him less and less with each shovelful. The sound of the pounding dirt was replaced by a low-pitched hum. I was surrounded by darkness. I could not move.

I eventually detected the faint aroma of a cigar and inhaled the welcome fragrance deeply. I opened my eyes and saw Harry, standing only inches from me, primed to react.

This time I maintained total control of my emotions. I breathed deeply and brought myself back to the present gradually. I blinked several times. As my vision came into focus, I saw men in indigo Civil War uniforms, Union re-enactors, setting up their encampment around me. Several stood by their tents watching me curiously.

Harry removed Roy's walking stick before I realized I still clutched it against my chest and inquired, "You okay, Kate?"

I looked from tent to tent. Many of the gawkers returned to their chores. I swallowed my embarrassment and replied, "Yes, thank you, Harry." As we walked through the campsite to return to the waiting Allnutt family, I felt a line of Union soldiers' eyes upon me.

Roy's family was congregated around a stone bench beneath an ancient, ailing sycamore. My somber countenance must have warned them my news was not good. By this time, re-enactors and spectators covered the grounds like hungry ants at a picnic. To have some peace, Mark suggested we go into the main house to discuss my vision.

The death I had experienced only minutes before must have affected me acutely. As we passed the old stone barn that housed the lodge and restaurant during ski season, I felt compelled to stop. The Allnutts and Elliott watched as I lingered at the entrance to the lodge. That all-too-familiar queasiness overcame me and surged between my stomach and my throat. An eerie sense of foreboding hung in the humid air, and I tried unsuccessfully to conceal my shudder. The heat might simply have been too much for me. I was not, after all, a hot weather person. The thought crossed my mind suddenly: Perhaps I lacked the fortitude to handle this criminal investigation.

I felt better, however, shortly after entering the cool parlor. I concluded I merely could not tolerate the intense heat. Marjorie and Rowena graciously offered to make iced tea.

I rested on the loveseat still somewhat dazed. Harry accepted for both of us. As we awaited their return, Mark's dogs, Charlie and Snowball charged down the staircase and into the room. They naturally greeted Mark first. Then they made a beeline for me.

I was delighted to see them again, and hugged them both tightly. I was rewarded with canine kisses. The touch of their coarse fur and their earthy scent helped ground me. I felt much better.

Sheriff Hobart offered Mark's dogs treats that he produced from his uniform pocket. Charlie and Snowball accepted the biscuits jubilantly, and Hobart stroked both dogs as they ate. Harry watched Hobart's interaction with Mark's dogs then looked over at me and winked as if to indicate we might have misjudged the sheriff. I, however, reserved judgement. I was thankful Charlie and Snowball's presence had shattered the tension that had enveloped the room.

Marjorie and Rowena returned with the a silver serving tray filled with drinks. I sipped my iced tea then proceeded to describe what I had seen at the pond. Marjorie assumed everyone was preoccupied with me, and reached for the sherry decanter. Unfortunately, Victor saw her and removed her savior from her grasp. He handed her a glass of iced tea without comment. Marjorie wrapped her tiny hands around her glass and marched to the window seat where she plopped down like a disappointed child.

All eyes were riveted on me as I revealed each detail of my vision. I was the only one who noticed both dogs strolling about the room . . . watching, listening, smelling. They inched their way into the hall and sniffed intently Roy's walking stick which Harry had propped against the gaming table. I thought it odd that the dogs tracked directly to Elliott and sniffed his right hand which rested on his knee. Elliott's affection for the dogs was evident as his stiff mien softened. He placed his glass on one of the coasters on the tea table, then patted each dog's head, and rubbed each muzzle. Charlie and Snowball appeared satisfied. They trotted to Mark and curled up at his feet. Elliott's attention returned to me, and he resumed his rigid posture.

I had barely finished when Elliott asked in an officious voice, "You still have not positively identified the man in the pit as Roy. Isn't that correct, Katherine?"

I felt as if I were in a witness box being cross examined. "That is correct."

"So actually you have given us nothing solid to go on." Victor added. He raised his left brow, then fixed his icy gaze on Sheriff Hobart. "And keep in mind, sheriff, you found nothing when you and your men searched the area where Charlie and Snowball found Roy's stick."

Mark joined the pack as it attacked its prey, "Hell . . . we can't be sure exactly where my dogs found Father's walking stick. Your theory that they found it at the pond is purely conjecture, sheriff."

"Conjecture based on years of experience," Sheriff Hobart rebutted as he slammed his glass onto the tea table spilling a quarter of its contents. Marjorie hurried to the table and nervously wiped the spill with her napkin.

Harry rose from his place next to me on the loveseat and moved ponderously to the center of the parlor. He locked his hands behind his back and rocked repeatedly from his heels onto his toes. When he had everyone's attention, he spoke. "You Allnutts asked Kate . . . uh, Katherine, and me here today to try to help you uncover information about Roy's disappearance. In my humble opinion, Katherine has done exactly what you asked." Harry glanced at me approvingly. "I am sorry if you think Katherine has failed. However, I disagree. She has provided you with valuable information. If what you espouse is true and you seriously want to uncover the circumstances surrounding Roy's disappearance, you will stop maligning those who are trying to further this investigation."

Bravo Harry! That clan deserved your tirade. Colin

always said I was surgically precise. He should have witnessed this.

Rowena walked to the middle of the room and stood next to Harry, her hands clasped at her bosom as if in prayer. "You are absolutely right, Harry, of course. I am certain Mark, Uncle Victor, and Elliott are simply venting their frustration. They did not intend to criticize Katherine or Sheriff Hobart." Rowena circled the parlor, her arms outstretched as if to encompass everyone present. "I know I speak for all of us when I tell you both how very much we appreciate your assistance."

Sheriff Hobart stood up and rested his gun hand on his holster. "I think we might have uncovered something here this morning. I should be getting back to my office. I've got to send Roy's stick to the forensics lab in Harrisburg." After the sheriff seized Roy's stick from the hall, he pointedly exchanged glances with each person in the parlor . . . except Harry and me.

Cursory goodbyes were exchanged at the door. The family's remarks made it abundantly clear Harry and my assistance was no longer required. We stepped outside, and the door closed promptly behind us. I turned around as we walked to my car to see if the Allnutts were watching. I saw no one at the windows, but I noticed a curtain in the parlor move.

Harry and I were seated in my station wagon and I had started the engine when Sheriff Hobart stuck his head in my window and asked, "Could you two follow me to my office? I'd like a word with you in private."

When we entered Sheriff Hobart's office, the heat and humidity were so pervasive it was like entering a sauna. He offered us the same seats we had occupied last Sunday, then leaned his back against the door and rapped Roy Allnutt's walking stick against his pants leg.

"Now that we are alone, tell me what you *really* saw."

I scratched my temple in amazement. What part of my

vision hadn't the sheriff understood? I had always prided myself on being an excellent communicator. I looked at Harry, who shrugged his shoulders, as I answered, "I saw and felt exactly what I described at the Allnutt's."

Hobart's body language screamed, "*That's it?*"

Since we were supposed to be on the same side, and Kenny Hobart was definitely not P. D. James's Adam Dalgliesh, I decided to be patient with him. "Sheriff Hobart, other than omitting the horrific sense of foreboding I experienced outside that old barn the Allnutt's use as their lodge, I have nothing more to tell you." I straightened myself in my seat and continued, "However, there is one question I have for you."

The sheriff strutted over to me and wedged his shiny black shoe between my leg and the metal chair arm. "And what might that be?"

"Who in Montaview could give us a real picture of the Allnutt family? And where can we find that person?"

His bewildered expression betrayed that was not the question he had expected. Hobart stood over me, his mouth agape, then finally answered, "You mean you think the Allnutts are hiding something?"

"We sure do, sheriff," Harry chimed in. "Every family has its skeletons. We want someone to tell us how many the Allnutts have and how much they want or need to hide them."

Funny, I had not entertained that possibility. Surely, my family had no skeletons. If it had, that would certainly be intriguing.

Sheriff Hobart walked over to his desk, flicked on the small rotating fan on the radiator, and sat down. Although the office was tiny, the air from the fan did not reach Harry or me.

The sheriff rested his chin thoughtfully on his left hand. He drew spirals on a note pad with a government-issue, black pen he gripped tightly in his right hand. "I really don't think the Allnutts have anything shady in their past," he said. "Other than the gossip about Roy and his women, the Allnutts have always been well respected in this community. They belong to all the civic clubs and donate a fair amount of money to local charities. Although, in the past few years, their donations have been getting slimmer and slimmer. But hell, money is tight for everybody nowadays . . . even the wealthy ones." He smirked, seemingly taking pleasure in the Allnutts' unfortunate reduction in cash flow.

I continued tenaciously, "Sheriff Hobart, can't you think of anyone in town who might know them more intimately." I suddenly realized the implication. "What I meant was a close friend of one of the Allnutts—or an employee perhaps."

"Well, old Pudd Gormley worked for the Allnutt family since he was a boy. Hell . . . Pudd worked on that farm when Roy's parents were still running the place."

Sheriff Hobart stopped doodling and looked across the room at the two of us. Perspiration dotted our foreheads. I could not speak to Harry's discomfort, but my fuchsia polo was sticking to my back. Even though his office was stifling, the sheriff did not appear bothered by it. Hobart continued, "But Pudd probably won't do you two much good 'cause Roy fired him about ten years ago. Pudd won't know anything about what's up with the Allnutts now."

Something the sheriff said must have suddenly struck a cord with Harry because he exclaimed, "Pudd Gormley! I remember him. He was a farmhand for the family when Roy and I were in college. I believe Pudd was a nice guy, but as I remember, Pudd drank more than he worked."

"Still does," Sheriff Hobart slapped his pen down onto his pad. "We stop him for DUIs about once or twice a month. If I had wanted to, I could have taken his license long ago." Hobart shook his head like a parent unable to control a disobedient child. "One of these days, Pudd Gormley's gonna wrap his old Chevy truck around some tree and kill himself."

I felt a sudden sense of urgency. "Where can we find Pudd? I would like to speak to him today if possible."

"He works as a groundskeeper at the Magic Mountain Golf and Country Club. He should be working today. Those spectators who come to watch the re-enactments don't realize the club's land abuts the Allnutt place. The spectators usually leave a mess near the golf course so the club management likes to have Pudd around to clean up."

"I think we should be on our way." As Harry and I headed for the door, I said, "Thank you, Sheriff Hobart. You have been most helpful."

The sheriff followed us outside and said, "If you two learn anything important, you'll let me know . . . right?"

Harry and I glanced at each other, winked and both replied, "Right."

My air-conditioned Volvo was a welcome relief from the sheriff's steamy office. While the cool air revived us, Harry and I decided our best course of action was to inquire about Pudd Gormley at the country club's main building. We did not want to waste time wandering around the golf course obstructing play and asking golfers if they had seen Pudd. Additionally, I thought it unwise to wander too close to the Allnutt property on the off chance a member of the Allnutt clan might see us and become suspicious.

The country club's receptionist busied herself at a stark but expensive blonde mahogany information counter. She wore a beige linen suit that blended nicely with the earth tones present in the furnishing and draperies. Her fine, naturally blonde hair was extremely short. Wisps rested on her ears and forehead, giving her elongated face the appearance of fullness. Her long fingernails were painted tangerine to match the lipstick painted on her narrow lips. Her posture was perfect, and she held her head high. Having been trained in classical ballet myself, I recognized her dancer's graceful hand movements immediately. She appeared young enough to be performing with a ballet company. I wondered what twist of fate had wrenched her from the stage and deposited her behind a reception desk at a country club.

She informed us in her mezzo-soprano voice that Pudd Gormley would be stationed at the back nine. Since we were not dressed for golf, she must have thought it her duty to check the soles of our shoes to ensure our heels would not damage the greens. Satisfied, she condescendingly pointed us in what I hoped was the right direction. We were about to exit when I realized I did not know what Pudd looked like. I hurried back and asked her to describe him.

She replied curtly, "The man's given name is Renson Gormley. Pudd is his nickname. Believe me, when you see him, you will know why."

Harry and I made our way to the back nine which lay dangerously close to the Allnutt property. The boundary between them was the hemlock grove bordering the Allnutt pond.

I recognized Pudd immediately. The leviathan reclined beneath a brilliant red maple. A black plastic trash bag draped over his paunch and his work gloves covered his face. Pudd must have heard our footsteps on the parched grass. Before we reached him he dragged his bulk up and pretended to be scanning for trash.

"Could we have a word with you, Mr. Gormley?" I asked.

"I'm awful busy here," he said, his small, pig eyes peeking out at me from under his grimy John Deere cap. His speech was slurred. "But I guess I could stop . . . but just for a minute or so. Hear?"

Pudd Gormley was aptly named. His spider-veined, bulbous nose and his fleshy cheeks mushed together like a pudding. His entire face changed shape whenever he moved his mouth, which to my dismay, he did with regularity. Pudd chomped . . . then spat . . . then chomped . . . then spat . . . chewing tobacco. His sun-parched lips were stained brown. All of his teeth were likewise discolored—except his incisors—they were missing. Had his face been slightly more sunburned, he could have been mistaken for a giant Halloween jack-o-lantern.

Harry grimaced. I thought Harry's reaction odd considering his lackadaisical attitude toward his own appearance. I glanced at Harry disapprovingly, and Harry cut to the chase. "We were told you once worked for the Allnutt family at the Magic Mountain Ski Lodge."

Pudd drooled tobacco spittle. "Yep." He wiped the juice from his chin with his rough hewn hand and smeared it on the leg of his faded green bib overalls. "Would still be working there if that son-of-a-bitch Roy Allnutt hadn't up and fired me for no reason."

This had the makings of exactly what I wanted. I replied in a feigned tone of regret. "Oh, that is a shame, Mr. Gormley. I cannot understand why anyone would fire an exemplary employee like you."

I think Pudd was thrown by the word exemplary because initially he stared blankly into space. But then as if the word's meaning miraculously came to him, or more probably he no longer cared, Pudd turned himself toward me. Pudd removed his cap and wiped the sweat from his brow with his hairy forearm. "I didn't understand it either. Now mind you, ole Mr. Allnutt, Roy's daddy, and I got on just fine. Same with the rest of um. But Roy and I started buttin' heads the minute he came home from college and talked his poor daddy into turnin' that fine ole dairy farm into that damn ski lodge." Pudd's voice filled with vinegar, "Roy kept me hoppin' from sunup to sundown. I decided if I wanted to keep my job, I'd best keep my mouth shut. So, that's what I did. And I stayed on there quite a few years after Roy took over."

"When were you unjustly fired?" Harry kept up the pretense as he lit a cigar.

Pudd spat, but this time a wad of tobacco landed on his

weathered, work shoe. He kicked the tobacco into the grass and continued, "Let me think here a minute. It wasn't long after Miss Rowena got real sick with that, uh . . . uh . . ." He snapped his dirty fingers and looked heavenward for the word he needed.

Pudd would never have been mistaken for a lexicographer. I took pity on the poor man, and assisted. "Diabetes?"

Pudd pointed a tawny finger at my face. I blinked and stepped backward instinctively.

"Yeah, diabetes." Pudd stopped short. He studied Harry and me cautiously. "I'm not sure I should say anymore."

"You can trust us," Harry coaxed, as he puffed intently. "We are old friends of the Allnutts."

Pudd looked around as if he was worried someone might be watching. He looked past us and into the hemlock grove.

Harry persisted. "How about a nice cold beer. There is a bar in the club."

"No, no! Not there." Pudd's eyes flew open. He suddenly appeared alert. "I get off in about a hour. I'll meet you at The Village Restaurant back in town. We can talk there."

Chapter 9

Since Pudd Gormley would be meeting Harry and me in Montaview in an hour, we decided to take advantage of that time and look around the Allnutt place.

Hoping to come upon something that would further our investigation, Harry and I melted into the crowd of spectators at the Union encampment so we could pursue our work undetected. Actually, the encampment was quite interesting. The re-enactors were extremely knowledgeable and eager to share their knowledge of everything from boot repair, and muzzle loading to field hospital protocol with anyone willing to listen. When the camp doctor pretended to amputate a soldier's arm, I had to turn away. I cannot stand blood. I can tolerate seeing my own blood; but seeing someone else bleed is another matter all together. While Harry and I moved from demonstration to demonstration, we both kept our eyes peeled for the Allnutts.

A half hour passed before a familiar voice came over the public address system. "Ladies and gentlemen, a tactical between the 27th Virginia Infantry and the 139th Pennsylvania Infantry will commence in five minutes on the field behind the Magic Mountain Lodge and Restaurant. Signs have been posted for your convenience. This is Elliott Danforth of the law firm of Billings and Newkirk, P.A., your proud sponsor of this exciting event. Thank you."

Elliott, like so many of us, must have been a creature of habit. His Jaguar was sitting exactly as it had been last Sunday. Today, however, Elliott was dressed in full Captain's uniform. Portraying a mere private was not Elliott's style. As usual, he was surrounded by his minions. Harry and I remained well to the rear of the crowd.

While we watched Elliott as living history Harry spied Mark marching toward the battlefield with the 139th Pennsylvania Infantry. If last weekend had been typical, Marjorie would be tipsy in the main house, and Rowena and Victor would be manning the gallery. Harry and I should be at liberty to have an unencumbered look around the grounds.

Harry followed me eagerly as I traversed the area between the encampment and the gardens. First, we reached the rear wall of what must have been the original smokehouse. Over the popping of the mock battle rifle fire, Harry shouted, "What are we supposed to be looking for, Kate."

I held my finger to my mouth to warn Harry to speak softly. I stretched my body against the grey stone wall and, with my forearm, urged Harry to do the same. "I am not sure what I am looking for. But when I find it, I will know."

Harry and I were flies clinging to the century-old building. The stones' rough edges scored my hands; but I did not mind—their dampness also cooled me. I touched the weathered wood of the smokehouse door. I gripped the rusty door latch and squeezed. The door opened with a mournful creak. I ventured in with Harry following close behind.

Remembering smokehouses have no windows, I commanded, "Do not close the d . . ."

Too late! Harry pulled the door shut behind him. I heard him take several steps to his left. We stood in total darkness. The air smelled of long-forgotten Easter hams, tar, and gasoline.

"Don't worry, Kate, I'll feel along this wall here and find the light switch."

Fumbling noises came from the direction of the door. Either Harry was groping for a light, or we had disturbed a huge critter's repose.

"How stupid of me, Kate. I'll use my lighter to get some light in here."

"Are you crazy?" I screeched. "Can't you smell the gasoline?" I turned and took three steps toward what I assumed to be the door. As my right foot took its next step it connected with the corner of some metal object on the floor which sprang up and smacked my shin. "Damn!" I said as I grabbed my shin.

"Are you alright, Kate?"

"I am alright, I suppose." I answered as I rubbed my shin. "I should have brought my flashlight from my car."

"I'll bet you have blankets, flares, and a first aid kit in your car, too."

"Of course I do, Harry. I think it is always wise to be prepared."

"But we don't have the flashlight now, and we can't wander around here in the dark. Let's get out of here before one of us gets seriously hurt."

I could not argue with his logic. After much banging and cursing, Harry found the door and opened it. The bright daylight was welcome; however, I empathized with Puxatawney Phil on Ground Hog Day as the unwary creature is roused from his sleep and thrust into unaccustomed light.

Harry shielded his eyes and stepped outside. I followed, then backed up to the wall immediately. When my eyes had adjusted to the light, I noticed Harry watching me. He said, "Kate, my beauty, I think you're carrying this cloak and dagger thing to extremes. No one knows we're here so why are we skulking around?"

"Oh, all right, Harry," I pouted. I found our detective work intriguing; however, I was probably unnecessarily concerned about being seen by the Allnutts. Perhaps I had missed my true calling. I should have been a FBI agent. The FBI had attempted to recruit many Accounting majors prior to graduation, but I had wanted to go into public accounting. How can anyone at twenty-one know what they really want to do with the rest of their lives?

Harry interrupted my musings, "Kate, where to next?"

I pointed toward the main house and said, "Since we took a cursory look in the lodge's windows last Saturday and saw nothing, let's move on to the summer kitchen. I saw Victor come from there this morning."

The exterior of the two-story former summer kitchen was grey stone like the Allnutt house. The freshly painted window sills and repointed chimney led me to believe it had been converted into an apartment . . . probably Victor's. Williamsburg blue curtains hung at the windows, and a painted milk tin overflowing with late-summer flowers sat near the narrow wooden door. I sent Harry around back to see what he could find while I peeked in the front window.

The interior beams had been exposed and the walls white-washed. Bunches of brightly colored dried herbs and flowers hung from the beams. Muted watercolors were displayed in antique frames. An old easel to the right of the immense cooking fireplace held a portrait of a young child in a burnished gold frame. Unfortunately, the light streaming in the window obliterated the child's face.

"Find anything?" Harry asked.

"Not really," I replied.

"As I was looking through the kitchen window," he continued, "I noticed a small, empty vial on the counter top. It was too far away for me to read the label." Harry paused and stared at the ground while he pushed a wisp of his thin hair off of his forehead. "I know it has been years since I worked in that vet's office, but the vial looked a lot like insulin to me."

"I wonder if both Rowena and Victor are diabetic?" I gave

Harry a nudge toward the front window. "Can you identify the child in that portrait?"

Before Harry could answer, something struck the wall beside us.

Harry and I dove to the ground as he yelled, "What the hell?"

We hugged the grass as we scurried like frightened lizards around to the left side of the building. I was amazed Harry could move that fast. I was uncertain whether the pounding in my ears was my heart or cannon fire from the mock battle. We crouched, waiting for another shot, but heard only the re-enactors' rifle fire. We waited what seemed like an eternity, but was most likely fifteen minutes, then crept back to the front of the building to examine the damage. I surmised a bullet must have struck the wall, and ricocheted off the stone because we found no bullet holes.

Harry lit a cigar and grumbled, "Some damned re-enactor had piss poor aim."

"Harry, don't you remember Elliott saying re-enactors never used live ammunition? Well, I am no expert, but that shot sounded like live ammunition to me." While Harry puffed I wiped the perspiration from my face with my handkerchief. I tried to fan myself, but it did not help. "Don't be so naive, Harry. Somebody knew exactly who they were aiming at—and it was you or me."

I decided this was not a good time to tell Harry of my recurring dream of being shot by someone wearing indigo.

*   *   *

The Village Restaurant was an old-fashioned luncheonette complete with metal pedestal tables with red and white marbleized Melmart tops. The cushions on the chairs and booths were red naugahyde. The cushion on our booth was cracked from age and, if the size of the present crowd was an accurate gauge, constant use. We saw no sign of Pudd.

Our aging waitress in a starched red uniform and white frilly apron was surprisingly accommodating when I informed her we were waiting for someone. She set out three white paper napkins and three place settings of uncomfortably angular stainless. She winked at Harry and treated him to a Las Vegas lipstick smile. She said, "Hot as Hades out there today, ain't it?" She did not expect or wait for our reply. "I'll just get you two something cool to drink while you wait. What'll it be, hon?"

As usual, Harry ordered Coke and I iced tea. Trudy, our waitress—identified by her plastic name tag and her gold ID necklace—spoke cheerfully to everyone along her path back to the counter. Although she was a spindly woman, she swung what little hips she had in such a come hither way, the men could not take their eyes off of her. I could tell from Harry's blank face, he had missed Trudy's move entirely.

I was beginning to feel we had been stood up when Pudd Gormley squeezed through the opened side of the double door. He gave and received numerous salutations and slaps on the back as he made his way to our booth. Realizing he would not fit beside either of us in the booth, Pudd pulled up a chair, and straddled it. I wondered if the chair would hold him.

When Trudy returned with our drinks, Harry and I ordered the soup-of-the-day which, luckily for me, was vegetable. Every other dish on the menu was either centered around meat or fried. From the greasy odor that had assaulted me the moment I stepped inside The Village Restaurant, I assumed the same cooking grease had been used repeatedly since the restaurant's opening in the fifties. Pudd ordered "the usual", and a Rolling Rock.

Apparently not wanting to appear too pushy, Harry kept the tone of our conversation light while we waited for our food. Pudd told us he lived alone in a cabin "up on the mountain", and it had belonged to his "greatgran' poppa". Pudd announced proudly that he had had plumbing installed two summers ago. From Pudd's appearance and smell, he had foregone the washing machine and shower. He rambled on about how much he liked the Allnutt children and how much he missed seeing them. Pudd flashed us his memorable smile when he said Mr. Elliott spoke to him regularly at the country club and kindly kept him up-to-date on Miss Rowena and Mr. Mark.

Then Pudd went on about Elliott "reachin' out and grabbin' his dream of bein' somebody . . . but not forgettin' his ole friends." He complimented Elliott on giving back to his community—not so much his time—but his money. Elliott "gave his money like most folks gave their advice".

In Pudd's opinion, Elliott also spent a great deal of money foolishly. Considering the source, I wondered if he meant Elliott wasted his money on matching knives, forks and spoons. Pudd shook with laughter when he told us about Elliott buying that maroon Jaguar to imitate Roy. Pudd commented that "foreign piece of junk" broke down almost weekly. He said the car was so bad that about three weeks to a month ago he had been driving home late one night when he had seen Elliott walking along a relatively deserted stretch of Route 15 North. Pudd naturally stopped and picked Elliott up. On their drive home, Elliott complained that his car had broken down on his way back from his firm's Frederick office. Pudd remarked that Elliott's mechanic must be "a damned fast worker" since he had seen Elliott drive his Jaguar onto the clubhouse parking lot at noon the following day.

The arrival of lunch stopped Pudd's chatter abruptly. I was surprised how quickly he turned his chair around to get a clear aim at the table. His "usual" turned out to be a hot roast beef sandwich with french fries. Both were smothered in gravy. The smell of the grease soured my stomach. As soon as Pudd's plate touched the table, he positioned his chin about an inch above it and commenced shoveling food into his open mouth. He took a breath only when he stopped to gulp his beer. Harry and I were so amazed, our soups grew cold as we watched Pudd's eating frenzy. The sound of Pudd's grunting and snorting prompted me to wonder how farm animals felt while feeding at a trough. Nothing evidently interrupted Pudd's meals so we waited until he gulped his last swallow of beer, leaned back in his chair, and belched before we asked about the Allnutts.

"I hope you enjoyed your meal," I began. "Now, getting back to the Allnutts . . . earlier, you mentioned being fired shortly after Rowena was diagnosed with diabetes."

"Yep."

I asked, "Could you explain?"

Harry finished his soup while Pudd told the remainder of his tale.

"Like I told you before, Roy and I never much got along. But after Miss Rowena came home from the hospital, Roy's ways turned real hateful. He snapped at everybody 'specially that poor Miss Marjorie. Seemed like every time I was walkin' past the house, I heard him yellin' at her. Callin' her all kinda bad names and throwin' stuff around."

"You stayed out of his way, right?" I asked. I had eaten all I wanted of my cold soup. Watching Pudd eat had diminished my appetite.

"Yep, as best I could. But this one day, I went on up to the house to ask Roy somethin' about the generator in the lodge." Pudd stared down at the table as if he was reliving that moment. His lips parted, but the words would not come. His normally gelatinous features stiffened. He eventually spoke in a strange, hushed tone, "When I was in the kitchen, I heard Roy cursin' at his wife real loud. She was sobbin' somethin' pitiful. I wanted to make sure Miss Marjorie was all right, so I barged on into the hall. I looked up and saw the two of um standin' on the landin'. Roy bent down and yelled somethin' in her face about her lyin' to him all those years. I remember Roy screamed, 'You never loved me, Marjorie. You only USED me!'"

Harry listened intently. "Have you any idea what Roy was referring to?" he asked.

"Nope. All I know is that tiny little bit, Miss Marjorie, kept on cryin' and tryin' to tell em somethin'; but Roy wouldn't shut his mouth long enough for her to get a word in." Pudd took a gulp of his untouched water and wiped his mouth with the back of his hand. "I remember Miss Marjorie blurted out somethin' about Victor."

Pudd shoved his chair away from our booth, jerked his head back, gazed at the acoustic tile ceiling, and threw his hands up. "Lord help her . . . Roy's eyes got all crazy." Pudd pulled his chair back to our booth, then he crashed down onto it. I thought I heard the wood crack. Pudd thumped his bulky elbows onto the table top, stretched his nonexistent neck towards us, and bellowed. "Roy Allnutt looked like the devil hisself!"

Harry and my astonished expressions must have warned Pudd to lower his voice. He surveyed the restaurant. Pudd sneered at the customers as he waved their curious stares away. "I've been in my share of barroom brawls . . . and I ain't never seen wilder eyes."

Without asking, Harry beckoned our waitress to our booth. "Another Rolling Rock for our friend, Trudy."

She returned promptly and proceeded to tilt his glass as she poured Pudd's beer from its bottle. The head swelled to the top of the glass so Trudy left the remainder of the bottle on our table.

Trudy dawdled, sensing a juicy tidbit of gossip might be forthcoming. She wiped a few nonexistent spills from the booth behind ours, and rearranged the utensils and napkins on the tables surrounding our booth. Pudd drank a third of his beer before Trudy gave up and returned to the counter.

"I thought Roy was gonna hit her, but he turned and walked down the hall. Miss Marjorie grabbed his shirt, I guess to try to stop him. Roy whipped around and backhanded her right across her face." Pudd wiped his sweaty brow with his tee-shirt's sleeve. "That sent Miss Marjorie flyin through the air." Pudd raised his right hand. "I swear to God I heard her bones crack when that poor little lady hit them steps."

I was stunned. "Didn't you try to help her?"

"Sure I did. I ran over and was gonna pick her up. But Roy charged down and pushed me away from her. I didn't think Roy had it in him, but he rammed me right into the front door. That crazy man's eyes were blazin'. He stuck his face in mine and hollered, 'Get out of here Renson Gormley and don't ever come back. And if I hear you've breathed one word about what just happened here to anybody, I'll KILL you!'"

Typically, Harry had to ask, "And did you tell anyone about it?"

"I'm still livin' ain't I?"

We thanked Pudd for the information. Harry left the money for our lunches on the table and slipped Pudd a twenty for his trouble.

As soon as we fastened our seat belts, Harry and I stared at each other and said in unison, "Victor?!"

Chapter 10

I hid my station wagon among the spectators' vehicles at the Magic Mountain Civil War re-enactment. The sounds of rifle and cannon fire comprised a discordant symphony, indicating another mock battle was in full swing. Everyone's attention was riveted on the fighting, so Harry and I dared to return to Victor's apartment—hopefully, unnoticed. The prospect of being a target twice in one day was unappealing.

Harry tried the latch on Victor's front door. It swung open, and Victor stood glaring at Harry like a storm trooper at a naive GI. I knew this might be our last opportunity to get inside, so I bent over quickly and grabbed my ankle pretending I had turned it. I hobbled toward Victor's door all the while moaning plaintively.

Victor rushed toward me. To my bewilderment, Victor swept me into his arms and carried me into his living room. With my face close to his, I detected a faint antiseptic smell underlying his Old Spice aftershave, and noticed an old cut along his chin line that was not healing well. Victor laid me on the camelback sofa and fluffed a tapestry pillow beneath my injured ankle. As he hurried off, Victor said in a soothing tone, "Just lie there, Katherine, while I get you an ice pack."

Harry peered in the doorway and threw his hands up . I waved him inside and motioned him to close Victor's door. Harry did so, but remained stationed at the door until Victor returned with the ice pack and offered him a seat.

Omitting the obvious question—why Harry and I had returned—Victor removed my deck shoe then wrapped the towel-covered ice pack around my ankle carefully. Victor perched on the edge of the sofa, "Do you think this will suffice, Katherine, or would you like me to take you to the hospital? My Jeep is parked around back."

"No . . . no, thank you, Victor. I am certain I will be fine." Harry sat at attention on the petite pointe chair across the room and grinned like an idiot savant.

My conscience was getting the better of me and I was about to confess to my deception, when Harry took command. "Thanks a lot for helping her, Victor. I know we got off to a rocky start."

"No need to thank me, Harry. It is the least I can do for both of you." Victor rose and paced in front of the enormous fireplace. "Please accept my apology for my behavior earlier today. I, I mean, we have been under such stress for so long, we are all a bit testy."

While Victor and Harry talked, I laid back against the cushion and perused the room. Every table was covered with photographs—pets, landscapes, wildlife. Family portraits adorned the mantle. From the clothing and hairstyles, many featured long-deceased relatives and friends. I could not help but notice that Rowena commanded more attention than anyone else—Rowena at college graduation, Rowena in full riding habit at a horse show, Rowena in grade school, Rowena in her christening gown.

Harry must have read my mind. Or, perhaps, I read his. He approached the portrait of the child on the easel and examined it carefully. After some time, Harry turned and looked directly at Victor. Harry left Victor no opportunity for denial. Harry said, "She has the face of an angel. This is Rowena as a child, isn't it?"

"Yes. The dear child has never outgrown her heavenly aura." Victor's frozen features melted like an ice sculpture in the sun. "I painted that portrait from one of her baby pictures." Unlike his brother, Roy, I believed Victor to be an insightful man. Victor sensed our suspicions and peered at the floor to avoid our questioning eyes.

The longer the silence, the heavier my heart grew for Victor. I bit my lip while trying to think of something appropriate to say.

Harry, good old Harry, went to Victor and put his arm around his shoulder. "You are Rowena's father aren't you?"

Victor sank onto a nearby footstool and hid his face in his hands. "How did you know?" Victor sighed. "Marjorie and I have tried so hard to keep this a secret."

With some maneuvering, Harry knelt down beside Victor. "It did not take Kate and me long to figure it out." Victor's hands dropped into his lap. Harry patted Victor's back. "If you love Rowena and Mark, the way I believe you do, don't you think it would be best for everyone concerned if you told them?"

The answer came to me before Victor could speak. I answered for him, "Rowena and Mark already know."

Victor's hands covered his heart as if to hold back a flood of emotions. His eyes asked what his lips could not.

"I have no idea when and how they discovered the truth," I said. "But is that really important now?"

"No, it is not, Victor darling," Marjorie replied as she stood in the kitchen doorway. She was the model of domesticity. I must have been so engrossed in my new-found revelation, I did not hear Marjorie enter by the kitchen door. "What is important is that we no longer have to lie." She waltzed in and sat on the sofa at my feet. A faint scent of sherry laced the redolence of her White Shoulders cologne. Marjorie fussed over my ice pack as only a mother could. "You poor little thing, does it hurt much?"

Guilt squelched my response.

"Now Katherine darling, you must let me fix you some tea. That will make you feel much better."

As she got up to leave, I tugged gently at her skirt. Swallowing several times, I ultimately said, "No, thank you, Marjorie. I am fine."

Victor stood and walked toward the sofa. He moved the petite pointe chair next to Marjorie. He sat, took her tiny hand in his, and pressed it to his cheek. Their affection appeared as bountiful as an autumn harvest. I longed to love someone that much.

Embracing Marjorie's hand, Victor said resolutely, "Marjorie, dear, our charade is finally over. We must tell Katherine and Harry the whole truth."

My heart stopped. I hoped the truth was not that Victor and Marjorie had murdered Roy. Despite my eagerness to solve the mystery I suddenly felt compassion for the two of them.

I glanced at Harry. He was still kneeling next to the stool, his hands folded piously on his belly. His mouth was a thin, straight line. The creases in his forehead deepened. I wondered if Harry's pained expression was a reaction to Victor's words or merely his own physical discomfort.

Marjorie cupped Victor's face in her hands. Her lips blew him a kiss. "As usual, you are right, my darling." Marjorie straightened in her seat and held her head high like a member of the Southern gentry she imagined herself to be. "I suppose I should start at the beginning."

Marjorie breathed a sigh pregnant with regret. "I have no earthly idea how else to say this." She looked to Victor. He nodded in approval. She appeared buoyed by his inner strength. "Victor and I were lovers in college. We met while I attended Hood, in Frederick, and Victor attended Mt. St.

Mary's, in Emmitsburg. We were so much in love," Marjorie cooed. "Victor was, and still is, an extremely talented artist. I had foolish visions of being the adored wife of a world-renowned artist. You know how young girls are . . . all I could see was the glitz and glamour. I was certain, with the right exposure, Victor's work could make us wealthy. I pictured us owning estates all over the world and hobnobbing with the rich and famous. I, of course, would return to my hometown of Charleston triumphant, having married such an important artistic figure." Marjorie simpered, "I must confess, my Daddy, God bless him, spoiled me terribly." She leaned toward Harry and me, and whispered, "Momma always complained that Daddy made me a helpless little dreamer. Well, I planned to show her that Daddy's spoiled little princess could do well for herself."

Victor rubbed his hands together pensively. "Marjorie ultimately realized this passionate bohemian was disinterested in money and power. I steadfastly refused to sacrifice my creative integrity to please anyone—especially a crass public. I was so young, idealistic, and stubborn." Victor studied his love with a reproving eye. "But my fatal mistake was bringing Marjorie here during spring break to meet my family."

Marjorie lowered her head in repentance. "Self-confident, big-man-on-campus Roy made a play for me. When he and I were alone, he spoke of his aspirations of wealth and position. Things I sought and Victor shunned. I must admit, I longed to share those dreams . . . but with Victor, not Roy." Marjorie picked up a photograph of Mark, Rowena, Roy, and herself from a gate-leg table. She ran her fingers over Roy's likeness barely touching the glass. "Roy was accustomed to getting his way. The day after the three of us returned to our respective colleges, Roy called me at my dorm at Hood. When I told him I could not see myself with anyone but Victor, Roy drove to Hood the following weekend to try to change my mind. I was flattered, but refused to see him."

"Naturally, Marjorie did not tell me about Roy's overtures." Victor's rigid jaw betrayed his brother's seduction of Marjorie still rankled him.

Marjorie spoke to the photo as if she were confronting Roy himself. "Roy persisted—phone calls, telegrams, flowers." She sighed and turned the photograph upside down on her lap. Marjorie clamped her hand on top of it as if to restrain it. She glanced sideways at Victor. "Within three weeks of our return from spring break, I discovered Victor and I were going to be parents." Marjorie walked to the table where she found the photograph originally, and turned it face down. She hurried back to her seat as if someone might reach out from the frame and grab her.

In a panicky, immature tone, she appealed to Harry and me. "What was I to do? If I married Victor, I was afraid we would be penniless vagabonds for the rest of our lives." She touched her painted fingernails to her color-coordinated, lower lip, being careful not to chip her nail polish with her teeth.

Victor defended her, "In retrospect, I cannot blame Marjorie for her actions. She and our baby deserved stability."

Marjorie must have thought Victor incapable of presenting the facts with what she considered sufficient emotion. With a quivering lower lip, she interrupted, "I knew Roy would be graduating in June, and thought he could give my baby and me the kind of life I had always dreamed of. So, the next time he called, I invited him to visit me at Hood. Roy and I began dating immediately." Marjorie folded her fingers and bowed her head like a novice beginning her prayers. She whispered, "I let Roy make love to me." Marjorie sat quietly as if she expected Harry and me to respond.

Our silence prompted her to continue in a sly tone of voice. "Roy was the type who needed to believe he had mesmerized me then whisked me victoriously away from his younger brother. I had to make Roy believe he was the father of my baby. I could not chance Victor discovering I was expecting so I broke off our relationship abruptly."

Marjorie stared at Victor, tears welling in her huge eyes, transforming them into soft tropical pools. "I remember every untrue word I told you. That I was intrigued by your older brother. That he represented the type of man I had always wanted. I even said I never loved you and never wanted to see you again."

Victor walked to the easel, draped his long, sinewy arms over the frame's edge and soughed. Suddenly remembering himself, he stood tall and said, "Naturally, I was devastated. The only woman I had ever loved and my only brother had betrayed me. My self-esteem was shattered. I left school and wandered around the country for months trying to find myself. I self-righteously blamed my family—especially Roy— for my problems. I cut off all contact with them. I settled in New Mexico eventually. I returned to my painting and pursued other artistic endeavors. I dabbled in woodworking and ultimately apprenticed under some of the finest master craftsmen in the country. As my creativity and self-worth blossomed, I resolved to establish a contact back home to learn news of my family. I wrote to Reverend Wentworth who had been our church's pastor since Roy and I were children. Reverend Wentworth and I corresponded for twenty or so years before I surmised Rowena was my daughter."

Harry looked perplexed. "You mean you never suspected that the child born five or six months after Marjorie and Roy's marriage could have been yours?"

"Actually no," Victor answered, his lips taut and nostrils flared. "I was traveling in the Southwest and knew nothing of Rowena's exact birth date."

Finding that questionable, I asked, "And when the good Reverend informed you of your niece's birth, were you happy for the proud parents?"

Victor leaned against the deep windowsill and gazed

outside for several moments before he answered. "I would be lying if I told you I was happy for them. At first, I was overwhelmed by jealousy and anger. All the emotions I had so laboriously restrained erupted." Victor turned to us and leaned against the windowsill. "I reminded myself that if I was to overcome my pain and get on with my life, I could not allow myself to indulge in hopeless speculation. So I concentrated on my work and wrote to Reverend Wentworth again when I felt emotionally strong enough to hear more news about my family."

Marjorie went to Victor's side and intertwined her arm in his. "Years later, Reverend Wentworth commented in one of his letters about the odd coincidence that both Victor and his niece were diabetic. Naturally, Victor was curious. Victor returned here unannounced on the pretense of establishing a woodworking and art studio in this vicinity."

Victor continued. "To my surprise, Roy and Marjorie welcomed me with open arms. Rowena and Mark bonded with me almost immediately. Although Mark masked it well, I came to understand that he suffered a lack of validation and encouragement from Roy. And Rowena—my seraphic rebel—seemed confused and hurt by Roy's sudden coolness and criticism." Victor's innate humility surfaced. "After several months, it became obvious to me I provided both Rowena and Mark with the fatherly support and understanding they needed." Victor's words were tinged with gratitude. "With them, I finally felt complete."

Victor patted Marjorie's forearm and sighed. "From the outset, Roy insisted I was welcome to stay as long as I wished. But I was torn. I knew I had no right to infringe on Roy's family life. However, Marjorie, Rowena, and Mark's uneasiness in my brother's presence was unmistakable. I debated whether to stay for days. Ultimately, I was convinced my instincts were self-serving. I came downstairs one evening to announce that I was leaving."

Marjorie added, "When Victor heard Roy in the kitchen raving at the children and me, he rushed to our defense. The two of them threw verbal punches first. That was the first time Victor allowed the hatred he felt towards his brother to surface. I was afraid they would come to blows. Fortunately, Roy was so drunk . . . like I should talk . . . he shoved Victor out of his way and stumbled out the kitchen door. Neither of us went after him. We were all relieved that Roy had gone. We heard Roy's car race down the lane as Victor tried to calm the children. Mark was such an introverted teenager, he refused to discuss the incident. And Rowena was in such denial she insisted on retiring and forgetting the whole horrible scene. When we were alone, I made Victor and me a cup of strong coffee. We sat at the kitchen table. Always the gentleman, Victor said anything and everything he thought might comfort me. When he was satisfied I was composed, he confronted me with his suspicions." Relief washed over Marjorie's troubled face. "The children and I were so terribly unhappy, I could no longer restrain myself. I burst into tears and told Victor everything."

Victor's quiet voice assumed a lethal tone, "I certainly could not leave them alone with that monster. So I stayed on and have protected them ever since."

I recall thinking as Harry and I said our goodbyes and walked to my car that I had gotten one of the things I had been asking for—a viable motive for Roy's mysterious disappearance.

Harry began to barrage me with questions the moment I started my Volvo's engine. "Did you hear Marjorie say . . .? Do you remember Victor saying . . .? Did you see Mark's expression when . . .? Do you recall Rowena's tone when . . .? What do you think Elliott meant when he said . . .?"

By the time I turned onto Route 116 and headed south toward Emmitsburg, I could tolerate Harry's harassment no longer. I turned to Harry and snapped, "Give me some time to think about everything that has happened today before asking me for my opinion. PLEASE."

I turned my attention back to the road just in time. I mashed the brakes to the floor and Harry was propelled toward the windshield. Fortunately, his seat belt restrained him.

"What the hell, Kate! "Are you trying to kill us?" Harry's voice sounded accusatory and tired.

"Of course not, you fool. You don't want me to hit that turtle in the road do you?" Without waiting for Harry's response, I jumped out of the car to retrieve the turtle before another car cruised around the bend and crushed it.

Harry squinted, trying to see the dark mound-like object in the dim light of dusk. Harry called to me, "That's not a turtle, Kate. It's a rock."

I ignored Harry, picked it up, and trotted back to my car. I shoved the *rock* in Harry's open window. Its legs swam desperately toward any solid surface, and its head swung from left to right looking for something . . . anything familiar.

"Here, hold it." I gently placed the box turtle on Harry's ample belly.

Harry lifted the turtle to examine it. It immediately retracted its head and legs. The turtle must have shared my aversion to Harry's stogie scent. Although, much as I hated to admit it, I was getting used to Harry's unsavory habit. The smell of his inexpensive cigars was uniquely Harry.

I closed the driver's door as Harry asked with a hint of teasing in his voice, "Are you planning to add this to your menagerie?"

As I considered the possibility, I started the car and continued driving toward the main road. "No. As much as I would enjoy sharing my garden with him or her, I think it would be best if this turtle remains in familiar surroundings."

I made a quick U-turn and drove to the stretch of road where I had found the turtle. I pulled onto the grass, and left the engine running. "If this is a female, she could have babies depending on her. This turtle belongs here."

Harry rolled his eyes.

"I'm serious, Harry."

Harry handed me the turtle obligingly. He remained in the car while I carried the turtle across the road in the direction it had been heading when I picked it up. The vegetation was so dense I looked for a stick to use as a makeshift machete and found the bottom portion of a broken limb that would suffice. I turned around to see Harry craning his neck to watch me hack my path through the brush. With each step, I slashed my way into an ever darkening passage. Rather than feeling wary of venturing with diminished visibility into unknown territory, I was exhilarated by the Eden surrounding me. My senses seemed heightened, and I was treated to an euphony compliments of the fauna's evensong. My verdant passage smelled of honeysuckle and pine, deer and fox. Suddenly, I found myself perched precariously at the top of a hill. Thinking the turtle would be safer in the brush at its foot, I decided to descend. I took several steps, and looked back to see if Harry had braved the wilderness and followed me. All I saw was the haunting ashen twilight painted on the ceiling of a cathedral of intertwined limbs. I shivered.

I climbed down the steep hill keeping the turtle pressed securely against my chest. I thought, for a moment, I felt the turtle's heart beating in unison with mine.

As I reached the midpoint, I felt the sensation of tumbling helplessly down the hill although my feet were still planted firmly on the hillside. The feeling was so disturbing, I stopped. I sat on the grass with the turtle resting comfortably on my lap and waited for the sensation to pass. Instead, it overwhelmed me. I envisioned an old truck veering off the road and careening down the hill where I sat. I caught a glimpse of a lone sticker on its rusty bumper as the truck passed by me. It read, "HOBART for SHERIFF". The truck plowed into a tree and burst into flames. The driver's limp body pressed against the horn. I assumed the blaring horn would rouse Harry. When he did not appear, I shouted, "Harry . . . Harry come help me!"

I left the turtle in the safety of the high grass on the hillside. I kept my eyes riveted on the burning truck as I ran down to try to pull the driver from it. As I approached the inferno, I paused to wipe the perspiration from my eyes. When my vision cleared, the flames, the driver, and the truck . . . had vanished.

Chapter 11

On Monday morning, I sat in my high-backed, tapestry desk chair with my mug of decaf Earl Grey tea in hand and surveyed my office. Every item was precisely as it had been since I had inherited this office from my predecessor. While I was comforted by the order I had imposed on my life, I found myself increasingly bored by it. I swiveled my chair around and gazed out my office window. Lately I had come to question the reality I had created for myself. I sipped my tea and watched an army of storm clouds invade the drab morning sky.

Last Saturday evening, I had staunchly refused to concede that my mind could have been overwrought from the events of that day, and that I could have imagined the old truck plummeting down the hill and crashing into the tree. At the time, the scene had seemed so real to me, I thought I felt the heat from the flames. Two days later, within my safe surroundings, I could still smell the truck's sweet, heady gasoline vapors and its acrid vinyl interior burning.

I took a deep breath and slowly exhaled. I smelled only lemon furniture polish and the bouquet of roses and lavender I had brought in earlier this morning from my cutting garden.

Time tends to bring events into perspective. In the

overcast light of Monday morning, I had to agree with Harry. Saturday had been arduous and had most assuredly taken its toll on both of us. The truck accident probably had been a horrible figment of my fertile imagination.

I sipped my tea and replayed last Saturday evening for the umpteenth time. Despite Harry's and my mental and physical fatigue, the remainder of our trip home had been a verbal frenzy of feelings and facts . . . accusations and defenses. We scrutinized each member of the Allnutt family in light of Roy's disappearance; or, if my instincts were correct, Roy's death. After much discussion and numerous attacks on each other's personal prejudices, Harry and I agreed that every one of the Allnutt clan had a reason to hate Roy and would benefit in some way from his death. Ergo, Victor, Marjorie, Rowena, and Mark were all suspects. Another thing we agreed on at the outset was that Elliott had no reason to want Roy dead. In fact, as far as Harry and I could determine, Elliott was the only person involved with Roy who genuinely cared for the man and, more importantly, who Roy had not wronged in some way either real or imagined. Why, then, did the mere mention of Elliott Danforth's name cause my stomach to knot? I bit my bottom lip. Perhaps I realized Elliott was too accurate a reflection of me.

I reclined in my desk chair and stared at the ceiling. As much as the circumstances irked me, Harry was correct in his assessment. Unless Sheriff Hobart sought Harry's and my assistance, we were no longer part of the investigation, if, in fact, the sheriff planned to continue investigating Roy Allnutt's disappearance at all.

I turned back to my desk and picked up my pencil. I tapped it on the stack of work papers awaiting my attention. To attempt to offset my disappointment, I resolved to be satisfied with the situation's advantages. First and foremost, I was rid of Harry Templeton. Although I had to admit I might miss him in some vague way. Second, I was free every evening this week to practice with Flute for the upcoming horse show. Third, I was not going to miss any more tennis matches with Ric. Not that I wanted or needed to be with Ric, but I usually enjoyed his company and tennis was excellent exercise. And fourth, my life would finally return to normal, and I could forget this insane Roy Allnutt business.

All day Monday and Tuesday my work, my dressage practice, and my home life went smoothly. Not one of my cats or dogs so much as sneezed. Usually, that was the way I liked it— no surprises. But by Wednesday morning a hint of ennui threatened the complacency I struggled continually to maintain. Even my morning cup of tea tasted bland. Should I have applied to the FBI when they tried to recruit me in college? Should I have pursued the sport of steeple chasing instead of having been content with the predictability of eventing? Should I have moved to Federal Hill, with its effervescent social and artistic climate, when Colin and I had divorced instead of remaining in sedate, conservative Catonsville? I gazed at the tea leaves left at the bottom of my mug and wondered why I couldn't read them. What flaw in my character compelled me to retreat to my safety zone the moment I found myself outside its boundaries? I felt like the turtle I had picked up on the road Saturday evening withdrawing into its shell when it sensed Harry's lap was uncharted territory. I wondered if I possessed the wherewithal to change.

The buzz of the intercom startled me.

"Katherine, a Harry Templeton is here to see you," Suzy announced in her nasal whine. "Are you available?"

"By all means, Suzy, send Mr. Templeton in." A tingling sensation began at my toes and rushed through my body. At the very least, Harry's and my bickering would invigorate me. As ghoulish as it sounded, I hoped Harry had come to inform me that Roy's body had been found, and Sheriff Kenny Hobart had again requested our help with the case.

Several minutes passed. No Harry. I rose and walked

toward my door to see what had detained him. As I reached for the polished brass knob, the door burst open. In bustled Harry clutching a large mug of freshly-brewed coffee he had undoubtedly cajoled Suzy into making for him. The aroma of strong coffee overpowered that of Harry's cigars. I surprisingly detected a faint starchy odor as Harry hurried by me and headed for my chair. Perhaps Harry had ironed his shirt. I stared at him. I believed he had. However, the wrinkles betrayed Harry still had not bothered to press his khaki suit.

Harry plopped himself down, stretched back, and put his feet on my desktop. I closed my door and leaned my back against it. Except for the coffee I had refused to make Harry during our first encounter, I felt trapped in a snowless globe of *deja vu.*

"How is Hathaway?" I thought Harry's cat was a safe topic to pursue.

"He's great!" Harry waved his arms to silence me. He continued soberly, "But my wonderful feline is not what I came here to discuss." Harry gulped his coffee and peered at me over the top of his glasses. As hot as that coffee appeared to be, it was a wonder he did not scorch his throat. As my mother always said, "No sense, no feeling."

Harry rested his mug on my work papers and announced, "Sheriff Hobart called me at my office this morning to advise me Pudd Gormley is in Gettysburg Hospital."

"What?"

Harry again waved me into silence. "Patience, Kate my beauty, patience." Harry removed his feet from my desk and retrieved his mug. This time he blew on the coffee before taking a hefty swallow. My dad had habitually blown on his coffee before drinking it, but I never understood how that single puff could have been an effective coolant.

"Hobart said last night one of his deputies was on his way home when he spotted smoke billowing from the woods off of Route 116," Harry continued. "With the dry weather they had been having, the deputy was afraid the fire might spread, so he alerted the fire department and then went to investigate. He found Pudd's burning truck smashed into a tree at the bottom of a hill. Fortunately, the deputy was able to pull Pudd out of the truck before it exploded. When the fire company arrived, their emergency medical team stabilized Pudd and rushed him to the hospital. Hobart told me he and his deputy had assumed Pudd was drunk and fell asleep at the wheel."

Harry gulped more coffee then removed a cigar from his suit jacket. He smelled it like a dog sniffs its bone. Harry ceremoniously clipped the cigar's tip and stuck it into his mouth. He lit the brown-leafed weed and puffed contentedly.

I closed my eyes and shook my head. I knew prodding Harry to continue with the details would be fruitless. He finally said, "When Pudd regained consciousness, he swore he had only had one beer. He insisted someone had pulled up next to him on the curve then swerved their car towards him and grazed the side of his truck. Pudd insisted he fought his steering wheel but lost control. He said his truck ran off the road, plummeted down the hill, and slammed into the tree. Hobart said Pudd's truck was a mess to begin with and since it had been so badly burned he could not determine whether there were any grooves from the car that supposedly swerved into it."

I was stunned. I sank into the wing chair next to my book shelves. "How is Pudd?"

"He has a concussion, some minor burns, and several cracked ribs. The doctors think he will be hospitalized for a while, but he should make a full recovery." Harry carried his mug with him as he rose and walked toward me. He stood squarely in front of me, leaned forward, and touched my shoulder gently, "Did you hear what I said, Kate?"

I looked up at him, "Of course, I did."

"Then you heard what I said about the accident occurring at the curve along Route 116?"

My facial muscles tensed at Harry's implication. I shuddered in disbelief. "You do not think my vision last Saturday evening was a premonition of Pudd's accident . . . do you?"

"Do you have a better explanation?"

I suddenly felt deathly cold. "Not at the moment." Harry handed me his coffee mug. I sipped his black coffee. It's bitterness rivaled that which was beginning to seep into my memory. I clutched Harry's mug and spoke as if I were in a confessional. "When I was in grade school, I began envisioning incidents—specific people dying, accidents, murders. Then . . . a few days . . . a week after I had one of those visions, I would read or hear that similar incidents had actually occurred. At first, I told my mother about my visions. Aren't children supposed to be able to tell their mothers anything?" I swallowed more coffee. "Naturally, she made light of them. She said, in her sarcastic tone, 'Katherine, you have been reading entirely many of those Nancy Drew books.'" With each word, my right hand twisted my blouse collar tighter.

I stared through Harry and into my mother's omnipresent face. "But as my predictions became increasingly more accurate, mother insisted she would no longer listen to my ravings. She said they made her nervous." My palms perspired. I handed Harry his half-full mug, and I wiped my hands on the linen handkerchief I carried in my jacket pocket. "After that, I simply kept my visions to myself. I suppose I could have told my dad, but that would have caused more friction between dad and mother. Of course, I told no one outside our immediate family." I chewed the inside of my lip and rolled the handkerchief between my fingertips. "As time went on, I learned to ignore most of my visions. They eventually all but disappeared. Until I had the vision about Luke."

Harry leaned forward again. This time, he grasped both my shoulders firmly. "Right, Kate, you couldn't ignore that vision, and thank God you didn't." Harry removed his hands from my shoulders. He took both of my hands in his. He gazed into my eyes and said resolutely. "You cannot, in good conscience, ignore this vision either. Kate, you know in your heart Pudd's accident had something to do with Roy Allnutt's disappearance."

I tried to find an objection hidden somewhere in Harry's eyes. I ultimately agreed. "You are right, Harry. But what do you propose we do about it? Remember, the Allnutts made it clear they no longer wanted our help, and Sheriff Hobart changes his mind as often as he changes his socks."

With an impish grin, Harry remarked, "I was not aware you were acquainted with Kenny Hobart's personal habits." Harry knew exactly how to lighten my mood.

I threw Harry's hands into the air. "I am not familiar with anything about Sheriff Kenny Hobart . . . you fool." I rose from my chair abruptly, and Harry backed away from me. I brushed past him and retrieved my purse from my bottom desk drawer. To Harry's surprise, I hurried over to him and intertwined my arm through his. We both laughed as I whisked my portly partner out of my door. In the privacy of the empty hallway away from Suzy's incredible antennae, I leaned over and whispered in Harry's ear, "As you are so quick to remind me, Harry, we must be patient. If and when the culprit makes another move, our help may be requested. Now . . . what do you say about an early lunch?"

"I would love to, Kate, my beauty. My treat!"

*   *   *

After I returned from lunch with Harry, I began to review work that awaited my signature. I was recalculating several entries the supervisor had flagged as possible discrepancies when, suddenly, the letters H-O-B-A-R-T flashed into my mind. Try as I may, I could not get the word out of my mind.

H-O-B-A-R-T followed me through every set of papers and home that evening. I was not thinking of Sheriff Kenny Hobart—but the word "Hobart". Those six letters imposed upon my quiet moments with my animals and, later, invaded my dreams. Perhaps the blue cheese dressing on my luncheon salad had not been fresh. Perhaps Harry and I had spent too much time talking about Sheriff Hobart and our case.

H-O-B-A-R-T! Those infernal letters haunted me the remainder of my work week. Friday, at five p.m., I decided that since I had practiced dressage with Flute every evening this past week, I could forego riding and would drive home directly from work. In the sanctuary of my own home, the St. George animal shelter, I would be able to relax in the company of my motley crew and try to determine why I could not erase H-O-B-A-R-T from my mind.

I sat in bumper-to-bumper traffic on the parking lot Marylanders resignedly refer to as the beltway listening to Loreena McKennitt's rendition of "Greensleeves" and mused. Mrs. Huziej usually shopped for groceries on Fridays. A fresh eggplant concoction over angel hair pasta would make a delightful dinner, and I would have five Lorna Doone shortbread cookies for my dessert. Five cookies a day contained all the extra calories I allowed myself. I vowed years ago to remain a size 6, and I had . . . much to the chagrin of my college chums. I would curl up after dinner with *Jude the Obscure* and make an early evening of it.

An hour later, I turned onto the road leading to my home in Oak Forest. The Forest, as the locals referred to it, was a small community of quaint cottages constructed primarily of either stone or stucco. Most of them rested among the dense trees which lined the entrance to Patapsco State Park. The pleasant sounds of birds and animals was interrupted only by an occasional vehicle heading toward the park. On spring and summer evenings, Oak Forest residents contented themselves with gardening, walking their dogs or an occasional cat, and jogging. For some unknown reason, every garden boasted an abundance of azaleas in addition to the foxgloves, hollyhocks, and phlox typically found in cottage gardens.

I stopped my car at the foot of my driveway to collect my mail. I wondered why merchandisers sent so many catalogs. I continued slowly up my driveway past the huge holly which stood as the centerpiece of my front lawn. I glanced at my house and thought I saw a large object sitting among the shadows on my front porch. The afternoon sun touched the corner of the porch where the object sat as I followed the driveway to the right of the house. In the hazy light, it appeared to be a large basket of flowers.

A gift from the surgeon I stopped seeing a month ago? I had told him I wanted only a casual relationship after my recent divorce. He confessed he wanted something more. I remember confiding that I needed time to find myself before I would be ready to share myself with someone. What I failed to mention was my confusion as to whether I would ever be ready for that type of commitment. We had shared our parting conversation over a lovely candlelight dinner on one of the porches at Pearce's Plantation. A single rose in a crystal vase decorated our table, and the night smelled of wisteria and honeysuckle. He had been the consummate gentleman and said he appreciated my candor and understood my position. Perhaps he simply wanted to touch base. How sweet.

I parked in the carriage house as usual. I opened the arched, wooden gate in the clematis-covered wall and entered the kaleidoscope of my garden. Bee balm, columbine, lamb's-ears, and hollyhocks bordered the stone walkway leading to the rear door. The pear tree was still heavy with fruit, but I spied several bees sampling an over-ripe pear which had fallen onto the lawn.

When I unlocked the door, I was greeted by Tristan's,

Ninianne's, and Cedric's wagging tails as the dogs rushed past me and into the yard. The cats followed me anxiously as I made my way through the kitchen and hallway and into the library where I deposited my purse and briefcase. Each feline wanted me to demonstrate the admiration he or she rightfully deserved as soon as my baggage touched the desk. I complied immediately. With their appetite for adulation temporarily satisfied, I hoped I would be forgiven if I retrieved my flowers from the porch before feeding them.

I opened the wooden front door and stepped onto the stone porch. Condensation glistened on the stones and made them appear to be flecked with mica. I thought at first glance the glare from the sun streaming onto the far side of the porch had distorted my vision. But my gift became more recognizable the closer I came. I had, in fact, received a basket of flowers . . . a huge white rattan basket filled with shriveled and dying flowers—a used funeral arrangement.

I was unamused by someone's bizarre idea of a joke. Probably it was Ric's offbeat way of reminding me of a favorite author's passing. I removed the card peeking out from the purple bow. The card felt hot from the sun. It read, "Stay out of other peoples' business!"

My eyes were transfixed on those words. My body stiffened. My breath would not come. I have no idea how long I stood there before I realized my dogs were barking frantically. I dropped the card and backed away from the basket. Was I being watched? I forced myself to take a deep breath and repeated, "This is merely a macabre prank . . . and I have nothing to fear . . . This is merely a macabre prank . . . and I have nothing to fear." But instinctively, my bowels churned, and my mouth went dry and acrid. I fought the urge to vomit.

Despite my mantra, I was afraid. I could not make myself turn my back to the road. I backed toward my door. When I felt the strength of the carved wood behind me, I groped for the wrought iron latch. I was steadied by the unwavering metal in my grasp. I swung the door open and hastened inside—never removing my eyes from my lawn or the road beyond. I slammed the door behind me. My violent movement and the unaccustomed noise scattered my cats. My heart thumped in my ears; my palms felt clammy.

Fearful my dogs might be in jeopardy, I ran through the house and onto the enclosed, rear porch. I peered through the screened door. I could not see them, but heard the three of them somewhere behind the carriage house still barking and growling fiercely. I retrieved an old riding crop hanging from a hook on the wall and raced to the carriage house. I heard angry screeching intermingled with the canine cacophony as I rounded the corner of the building. My dogs jumped and clawed wildly on the trunk of an oak. My eyes followed the trunk up to its summer foliage. There, on a crooked branch, I saw an irate squirrel cursing vehemently at my dogs. I called the dogs to me. They were engrossed in their pursuit and ignored me at first. But, eventually they came and sat by my side. Relieved, I hurried them inside.

My heart continued to pound like a tribal drum. I sat at the kitchen table with a much-needed glass of spring water. I alternated between sipping the water and chewing my lip as I thought about my options. My instincts told me the gift was no joke. Should I call the police? No! I would be too embarrassed to explain why I believed someone was threatening me. Why should they believe me anyway? Should I call Ric? No! He would think I was over-reacting; and considering it was Friday evening, Ric was probably out. My only viable option was to call Harry Templeton—but, after I fed my motley crew, of course.

When my companions were finally satisfied and happy, I mustered enough courage to retrieve the telltale card from my porch. I thought it strange that an hour of lying on the damp stone had not cooled the card. I dialed Harry's number.

"Harry, this is Kate . . . Katherine St. George. We need to talk."

"Hi, Kate. Hold on a minute." Harry munched something as he spoke. "Hathaway and I were having a bite to eat." By the sound of it, Harry was crunching either lettuce or a potato chip. Probably the chip. "What's up, my beauty?"

I told Harry about my unsettling gift. As I read him the card a sour taste crawled up my throat and into my mouth. My body twitched. I was relieved I had not eaten.

I heard Harry gulp something liquid. "It appears somebody wants you and me to remove ourselves from the Allnutt case. That card is an incentive for us to do just that."

Harry's resignation fired my determination. "First, the basket was left on my porch, not yours, so there is no need for you to take the threat—or whatever it is—personally. Second, this proves that somebody has something to hide, and he or she believes I am close to uncovering it. That's why that person is trying to frighten me."

"Well . . . that person is doing a damned good job of scaring one of us." Harry exhaled into the mouthpiece. His voice was unnaturally grave. "Be reasonable, Kate. That person probably murdered Roy Allnutt. Do you think he, or she, would think twice about murdering you or me?" Harry gave me no time to answer. "Kate, listen to me. I'll bet Roy's killer thinks you are closing in and feels trapped." Harry's wife's death must have flashed through his mind because he heaved a mournful sigh. "Remember, I know from experience someone in that position is capable of anything." Harry cleared his throat, but his voice groaned with pain. "Believe me . . . I have been on the crime beat for years. I've seen it all." Harry bellowed, "Kate, I'm telling you, for your sake—and mine—we must back off. Let the professionals handle it."

My jaw tightened with disappointment and resentment. "But, what if the professional—in this case, Sheriff Kenny Hobart—is Roy's murderer?"

"What makes you suspect him?" My assertion evidently caught Harry off guard. His tone smacked of skepticism. "How would Hobart benefit from Roy's death?"

"I don't know, Harry." My mind searched desperately for a plausible answer. I chewed the inside of my lip. "Perhaps someone hired Hobart to murder Roy and dispose of his body. Then, when I came into the picture and was able to describe the details of Roy's murder and burial, Hobart decided to use his position to thwart the investigation."

"I don't buy that, Kate. You may not like Sheriff Hobart, but I think he is a straight arrow. Besides, if my memory serves me, when you had your first vision, you said the person who bludgeoned Roy was short and stocky, which does not fit Hobart. And you didn't say the assailant was male."

My mounting frustration prompted me to ask the question which was more for my benefit than Harry's. "Then why does the sheriff's last name keep invading my thoughts?"

Harry's voice became strident. He took aim and fired. "How the hell would I know, Kate? Maybe you have some subliminal urge to burst out of your priggish veneer and experience a man who lives in the real world."

His words wounded me as my mother's had years before. I would not allow myself to be reduced to tears by my mother . . . or by Harry Templeton. I would not let my pain satisfy either of them. Self-control had always been my shield and caustic words my weapon.

"I can see this conversation is going nowhere," I said. "I intend to drive to Montaview tonight to look around and ask Sheriff Hobart a few questions. Are you coming with me?"

"No, I am not!" Harry's voice became bellicose as he continued his assault. "Do you realize no concrete evidence has been found to substantiate any of your so-called visions?"

My lip quivered as I replied, "You are forgetting Roy's walking stick."

"Probably coincidental." Harry battered me. "And those silly bells and saws you keep hearing in Emmitsburg—what the hell do they mean?"

"I have not pieced all those clues together yet." My voice assumed a childishly high pitch. "The scenes I envision, the feelings I experience, and the sounds I hear do not come with a user manual, Harry. I wish they did."

"Look, Kate, I could not risk telling you before, and I do not want to hurt your feelings now. But I don't believe in psychics—never have—never will. I was desperate to find my friend, and you supposedly found that police dog, Luke. I sought you out as a last resort." Harry puffed his cigar and reloaded his weapon. "You were a long shot that didn't pay off. I can accept that and so should you. Kate, stop playing cops and robbers before you get hurt, or worse yet, make a damned fool of yourself."

While Harry spit his insults, I breathed deeply and managed to control my seething emotions. When Harry finished, I said indignantly, "I have already made a fool of myself by listening to you in the first place, Harry. However, I am now involved in this mess, and I will see it through to its end." I spread my right hand across my chest. "I know in my heart Roy's body was buried near the Allnutt pond then moved somewhere else on their property. I must do whatever it takes to prove that." I took a half breath, then concluded, "I may very well be a fool, Harry, but at least I am not a coward!" I slammed the receiver into its cradle.

*   *   *

The route between Baltimore and Frederick seemed exceedingly long at 7:30 that evening. I kept fighting the urge to turn around and retreat to the security of my home. My entire life I had been afraid to venture outside my safety zone. Then, in the span of a few weeks, I put myself on the line for Luke, a police dog, and was about to put myself on the line for Roy, a presumed victim I did not know and probably would not have liked. My body trembled with fear and exhilaration. This was one of those rare times I felt truly alive.

After exiting onto Route 15 North, I glanced at the elegantly engraved business card I had placed on my dashboard before leaving home. Mrs. Huziej must have found it in my pants pocket when she had done the laundry and left it on my dresser. With all the commotion, I had forgotten I had taken it from Roy's Jaguar. I had noticed the card when I changed my clothes and brought it along.

The card read BILLINGS & NEWKIRK, P.A. Attorneys at Law. The name of the attorney issuing the card must have been on the bottom half of the card which had been torn off. However, hand written on the card's back, was the number 300,000. The handwriting on the business card matched the handwriting on the card with my funeral arrangement. Sheriff Hobart was not the only person I intended to interrogate this evening.

My short drive through Emmitsburg was filled with the harmonious sound of bells pealing. Since Harry had abandoned me, I had no one to ask if they also heard them. I passed a church, and stopped at the curb to look up at its steeple. The bells were still. The bells obviously rang only in my mind.

The drive west on Route 16 was as fragrant as it had been that first Saturday Harry and I had begun our quest. Yet this evening's humidity intensified each wild flower's scent a hundredfold. As the sun disappeared behind the mountains, the gun-metal grey clouds moving across the marbleized sky appeared burdened with moisture.

As difficult as it was for me to admit, I had grown fond of Harry. And, until today, I believed Harry had grown fond of me. We balanced each other as successful partners should.

There were moments I actually thought we had enjoyed each other's company. Why, then, had he hurt me? What had I done to make him turn his back when I needed him to stand with me? Worse yet, what besides self-centered arrogance lead me to believe I deserved Harry's devotion? Harry was not my father. Why was I so adept at business and inept at relationships?

Once again, where Route 16 intersected Chapelbell Trail, I heard bells. This time, however, the dissonant sound of a buzz saw overpowered the peal of the bells. I made a U-turn and turned onto Chapelbell Trail, having no idea what I hoped to find. Dusk settling on the dense woods cast eerie shadows on the narrow road ahead. My car's running lights reflected each drop of condensation which sparkled in the air.

Homes on substantial lots dotted both sides of the trail. A sign posted at the entrance to each driveway read NO TRES-PASSING—NO HUNTING. I drove past a cul-de-sac, know-ing instinctively I needed to drive around it. I backed up slowly and proceeded cautiously. Three driveways emanated from the cul-de-sac. The homes were not visible from the road, but their mailboxes sat at the entrance to each drive-way. Again, all three driveways were posted with that same warning. The first address was 2351 Chapelbell Trail; the second was 2353 Chapelbell Trail, and the third was 2355 Chapelbell Trail.

That last number, 2355, struck a cord. I wondered where I had seen those numbers before. My car idled in front of that driveway while I tried to remember. I sat there several minutes, but nothing came to mind. Surely it would not hurt to have a look at the house. Perhaps it would jog my memory. If I were caught trespassing, I would plead ignorance—a city girl who had lost her way.

The quarter-mile driveway snaked through a primaeval forest. Surrounded by such majesty, I felt insignificant. Eventually I reached a clearing. The mammoth, storybook chalet snuggled in the dell looked enchanting. The brightly lit, three-story house was adorned with gingerbread. The scene reminded me of my childhood in Baltimore where my parents religiously took me to see the Christmas window displays in the Hutzler Brothers department store on Howard Street. Sighting no cars, I thought it safe to continue toward the house. I assured myself the house lights were on timers.

Driving to within a hundred feet of the house, I stopped my car and peered at the floor-to-ceiling glass walls facing me. I thought I saw movement on the balcony in the great room. A masculine looking figure walked to its edge, then appeared to stare into the darkness. I switched off my lights and sat completely still . . . as if he could actually see me.

I felt perspiration collecting above my top lip. When I wiped it, I realized my palms were clammy. I did not need to be interrogated by a hostile homeowner or reported to Sheriff Hobart for trespassing. Without turning on my lights, I turned my wagon around and crept out of the driveway. When I looked back, I thought the house looked darker—my anxiety and overzealous imagination, no doubt.

Heading toward Montaview on Route 16, I decided to question Sheriff Kenny Hobart first. As I drove west on Main Street, I noticed the door to The Belfry was open, and Rowena was waiting on a customer. A Jeep was parked in front of the gallery; therefore, I assumed Victor was working with Rowena. I turned onto West Street. The sheriff's office was completely dark. Strange, I was under the impression that other than his dogs and hunting, Kenny Hobart had no interests except his work. I wondered where I might find him this time of night. Clueless, I decided to change tack and snoop around the Allnutt property where I would hopefully uncover some tangible evidence. Then I would be in a better position to confront the sheriff.

I turned into the entrance to Magic Mountain Ski Resort

and switched my car's lights to the low beams. If anyone was in the main house, I did not want them to see my car. Wanting to ensure a hasty exit, if necessary, I parked my car on the grass facing out toward the main road. I pulled my flashlight from under the rear seat and walked toward the Allnutt house. I felt assured that even if someone were at home, they had not seen my headlights in the rising fog.

I thought I should have another look around the out-buildings, but wanted to check on Mark and Marjorie's whereabouts first. I hid behind the smokehouse and looked for Mark's truck. The only vehicle present was an old Mercedes which looked like Marjorie's type of car. A light was on in one of the upstairs rooms. I hoped that was Marjorie's bedroom and, by now, she was a bit tipsy. The entrance hall and porch were lit as if awaiting someone's return—probably Mark's. I wondered if Marjorie sat up waiting for her children to come home the way my mother always had for me.

As I walked by the stone lodge, I experienced that same queasiness I had when passing it last Saturday. If I had learned anything from this escapade, it was to pay attention to my feelings. I moved to the lodge's Dutch door and tugged on its handle. It would not budge. I tugged harder. Nothing.

With determination, I stole around back and looked for another entrance. I fanned my light over the back wall. *Voila*— the fire exit. I engaged the lever in the door's metal handle, and the door sprung open. As I stepped inside, it occurred to me I might have tripped the building's burglar alarm. Hearing nothing, I quickly pulled the door closed behind me.

I dared not switch on any lights. My flashlight provided ample light to determine I was in a long hallway containing five doors. I wanted to find the lobby first, but I had no idea which door I should choose. I momentarily felt like the person in that short story *The Lady or the Tiger*. I gauged that the lobby door was straight ahead at the far end of the hall. As I hurried through the tunnel-like emptiness, I was haunted by the sense that I was about to be swallowed by a giant serpent.

I felt relieved when my hands pushed down on the door lever and it moved under my weight. I burst into the room like a child running from an unseen monster in a nightmare. The mustiness was oppressive. The fog shrouded moon shed the barest of light through the small windows—but enough to see I was precisely where I wanted to be.

I stood in the doorway with my arms outstretched as if I were bracing the door. I did not want to enter that room alone. But, I knew, that meant I must. To appease my fright and flight instinct, I propped the metal door open. I took several steps into the cavernous room and suddenly stopped. I thought I felt frigid fingernails clawing their way up the backs of my legs, my spine, and my head. I quaked. I told myself I was being childish.

I scanned the two-story lobby with my flashlight. The room boasted a cut stone fireplace that rose to the timbers of the roof. In an effort to maintain authenticity, the Allnutts had left the underside of the tin roof exposed. Cobwebs hung from the timbers like rotted shrouds from the mast of an abandoned ship. The registration desk and adjoining office were constructed of old barn wood which, if the lodge were alive with activity, would have provided a warm, cozy atmosphere. However, the smell of decaying wood, partially burned fireplace logs, and the specter of furnishings cloaked in tattered sheets gave the room a ghostly aura.

I walked among the relics of what appeared to have been a happier time. The plush carpets were rotting from rain dripping from the holes in the roof onto their natural fibers. I ran my fingertips over several items—a seating arrangement in the center of the floor, some fireplace stones, an empty baggage cart. Dusty. All the while, the letters, H-O-B-A-R-T, screamed at me.

The lobby sprawled into the restaurant's lounge. The tables were likewise covered in discarded linens. Several converted dairy stalls equipped with wooden benches in which romantic couples had stolen intimate moments amid the clamor of ski boots and mugs were now dusty and abandoned . . . probably like the relationships once fostered in them. Because the fireplace had been centrally placed, guests in the lounge were afforded the same opportunity to enjoy the fire as those in the lobby. I wondered why the Allnutts had allowed the place to deteriorate to its current state. Surely they could have found the money for its maintenance somewhere. Harry had said the Allnutts had been pillars of the community for generations.

I felt drawn from the lounge toward the restaurant. As I approached the restaurant's entrance, I passed a swinging door with a small, eye-level window. I was compelled to peek inside. My instincts shouted there was something in there I must see. The galley-like room was outfitted with steel commercial-sized appliances and a long, metal center island above which hung a large assortment of dingy knives and other cooking utensils. When I pushed the door open, it banged against the wall.

A putrid odor permeated the kitchen—probably standing water accumulated in a sink or a long-forgotten container of vegetables. My many years in horse barns and cleaning multitudes of litter boxes enabled me to tolerate unpleasant smells. However, the atmosphere in the entire lodge reeked of death—not necessarily of someone's flesh and blood, but of someone's aspirations and relationships—integrity and kinship.

I left the door open and walked around. I touched the steel counter tops and examined the empty plastic vegetable bins. I took down several utensils and cupped them in my hands. In my mind's eye, they evoked only visions of a hustling kitchen staff, and bountiful food and drink. I surveyed the kitchen with my flashlight looking for anything that might lead me to a clue. The manufacturer's name on the refrigeration unit across the kitchen suddenly caught my eye. There, in bold black letters, was the name–HOBART.

The closer I got to it, the more edgy I became. I tripped over several plastic weather mats rolled together on the floor. My stomach and throat tightened, and my normally cool hands felt frigid. Perhaps my fear of what I was about to find made me hesitate. I seemed to be moving in slow motion. I grasped the refrigerator's handle and was about to pull the door open when, behind me, I heard an all-too familiar voice. It said, "Katherine, if I were you, I would not open that door."

Chapter 12

I reeled around and shined my flashlight in the direction of the voice, but I already knew who it was. Elliott Danforth stood akimbo in the doorway. He was dressed entirely in black. Elliott's head appeared suspended surrealistically in midair as his body melted into the darkness surrounding him.

Elliott raised his right hand to shield his eyes from my light. He was holding a dark, metal object in his hand. He demanded in an overly calm yet alarming tone, "Katherine, remove your light from my face. You are not trying to blind me, are you?"

I braced my back against the refrigerator and inhaled deeply before answering, "Of course not, Elliott." I moved my light from his face and aimed it at the wall to his left. "What brings you out here this late?"

"I noticed your station wagon in my driveway and decided to follow you." The offset light made Elliott's smile appear more cunning than usual. "Don't look so surprised, Katherine. Since I first held your hand, I have remembered everything about you—the feel of your graceful fingers in mine, the look of your haunting amethyst eyes, the sound of your self-assured voice . . ."

Elliott lowered his hand and flicked on the metal

flashlight he held in it. As the light beamed onto the floor, it revealed a red gasoline can in front of his right foot.

It had been many years since I had run track in high school, but I knew I was still quick. If I doused my light and dashed for the door at the other end of the kitchen which, I hoped, opened onto the long hallway, I could probably escape before Elliott realized what was happening. Keeping my eyes fixed on Elliott's face, I took a step sideways.

"Don't you dare move, Katherine," Elliott warned, as he raised his left hand and pointed a pistol at my face. "You and I must have a chat about your troublesome interference."

I raised my sweaty hands above my shoulders obediently. "Certainly, Elliott, whatever you say." I was hardly in a position to argue. I needed to buy time to devise another plan. If Harry could see me now, he would certainly have the last laugh. Haughty Katherine submitting so readily.

Although I knew the answer, my ego tempted me to ask Elliott why he did not want me to open that refrigerator. But my mounting fear silenced me.

Remembering his grandfather's comment about Elliott's bad temper, I refrained from turning toward the door. Instead, I watched Elliott's every move. He stared at the open doorway intently.

"Tell us, Elliott," a gravelly voice asked the question I wanted to but would not, "what is in that refrigerator?" I recognized that voice immediately. Cocking my head slightly but keeping the rest of my body perfectly still, I saw Harry and Sheriff Hobart standing in the doorway. Someone behind the pair shined a light onto Elliott. My first response was relief . . . my second irritation. Harry should have realized Elliott was on the edge *and* in control. Tact was needed, not antagonism.

Elliott's nostrils flared and his lips parted. I noticed his pistol hand waver. Elliott answered Harry defensively. "He ruined all of my plans. The country club developers offered me a partnership if I could persuade the Allnutts to sell them the ski resort at a reasonable price."

A picture of the business card bearing the handwritten number 300,000 flashed into my mind.

As Elliott spoke, his eyes darted between Harry, Sheriff Hobart, and me like a guilty child's among three suspicious adults. "I mentioned the offer to Marjorie, and the greedy little mouse took the bait." Elliott threw his head back and laughed maniacally. "I made a metaphor! Miss Reitz, my old maid English teacher, would be very proud of me." Elliott howled with satisfaction.

I was sorely tempted to run toward Harry and the sheriff; but before I mustered the courage to take a step, Elliott abruptly stopped laughing, then continued, "Poor, lovesick Victor agreed to my proposal because he wanted to please Marjorie." Elliott moved his flashlight into his other hand. It dangled from his little finger, and its weight caused Elliott to fumble with his pistol. Then he shoved his index finger into his opened mouth, and pretended to gag. This was a side of Elliott that had been well concealed from everyone—especially the Allnutts.

Elliott curled his lip and snarled, "Mark bulked at first, insisting he wanted the old home place kept in the family. But ultimately, he conceded to his mother's wishes."

Elliott suddenly reverted to his normal self-assured demeanor. "Rowena . . . now she was a challenge. That spoiled little bitch flatly refused my offer. She thought she had me fooled. But I saw through her sickening sweetness. I knew from the beginning she spent time with me solely to regain Roy's attention and affection." Elliott paused, stared into the darkness surrounding him, then confessed. "I have coveted Rowena since the first time we met. She had such fine breeding. The Allnutt name was so well respected." Elliott looked at me, jutting out his chin defiantly. "I knew once we were married, I could force Rowena to accept the sale. So I pleaded with her to marry me. And, with Roy's urging, she accepted." The beam from Elliott's flashlight bounced off the blackness as he clasped his hands together and took several ceremonial steps toward me, mimicking a bride walking down the aisle.

Elliott shifted his gaze to me. "But you, Katherine, *you* are more to my liking. Your beauty, your education, your business acumen." He sighed. "Unfortunately, my plan was already in place. I couldn't allow anything or anyone to deter me."

I would have taken great satisfaction in slapping that smug grin from Elliott's face. Instead, I backed away from him. Janus-faced Elliott had duped everyone. I now understood my repulsion towards him. If I had listened to my initial instincts instead of listening to Harry, I would have been safe at home. But no, I was being held captive in an abandoned lodge by a homicidal lawyer. Where was the knight in shining armor my dad had promised would always protect me? I had hoped Colin would have been up to the challenge. He had tried, but he never quite fulfilled my expectations. Perhaps I expected too much. I chewed my lip as I juggled my flashlight from hand to hand. As I had always done when the world seemed too threatening, I wished my dad were here.

Sheriff Hobart stepped inside the door with his hands up and palms exposed. "Elliott," he said gently. "Look, I'm unarmed. I don't want to hurt you. I just want to talk. Lower your gun and let Katherine walk out of here. I'll stay in here with you, and we can talk this whole thing through."

"No." Elliott shook his head like a stubborn child. He waved his pistol at the sheriff and yelled, "Don't treat me like an idiot, Hobart. I can hear your deputies behind me. You want Katherine out of their line of fire so they can take me out!"

"No, Elliott," Sheriff Hobart continued, "no one is

going to shoot you. Just put your gun down. All I want is the truth."

"The truth? You want the truth?" Elliott switched his flashlight back into his empty hand and shined it at the refrigerator. He backed through his beam of light, and grasped the refrigerator's handle. He gave it a slight tug then moved away quickly. In his haste, Elliott slammed into the restaurant equipment lining the wall.

With the door ajar, the stench confirmed what was inside. Hobart's deputies entered from the door closest to Elliott, their service revolvers drawn. Elliott saw them and again pointed his pistol at me. He shouted, "I'll kill her! I swear I will!"

Sheriff Hobart waved his deputies off. The sheriff continued in a soothing tone, "Elliott, I know you want to tell us the truth about what happened. You started to tell us a minute ago. Let me try to help you, Lee. Did you put Roy's body in that refrigerator?"

"Yes," Elliott answered anxiously, like a child who was more worried about the punishment he would receive than the offense he had committed. "I moved Roy's body here after you advised the family that Katherine had envisioned someone bludgeoning Roy to death on the grass next to the pond. Katherine's visions . . . those damned visions . . . were exactly right." Elliott put his hands to his head and swayed back and forth as if he suddenly felt the pain he had inflicted upon Roy. "At first Roy agreed to the sale of the resort. Then he hedged and said he wanted time to reconsider. Roy was to give me his final decision in the hemlock grove late that night. When we met, Roy told me he had decided not to sell." Elliott's voice became louder and more agitated. "He went back on his word to me. That was the first time Roy had ever said 'no' to me. Roy tried to explain the reasons for his decision, but I was so furious I insisted he was wasting his time. Roy gave up. As he walked away from me, he dropped his walking stick. I shouted to him that I would never accept his decision. I resolved to make him change his mind. I demanded he stop. But Roy kept walking." Elliott glanced at me and frowned. "I have never allowed anyone to walk away from me without my permission . . . except you, last Saturday, Katherine." Elliott returned his attention to Sheriff Hobart. "I picked up Roy's walking stick as I ran after him." Elliott's eyes twitched and his mouth quivered. He appeared unable to speak. Finally, Elliott shouted, "When I caught Roy, I spun him around. We grappled. I hit Roy on the forehead with his walking stick."

Sheriff Hobart assisted Elliott. "And . . . you thought you killed Roy so you went to the implement shed near the pond and retrieved a shovel. Then you buried Roy in a shallow grave next to the pond."

Elliott began sobbing. "I was afraid. I didn't know what to do." Elliott rocked back and forth clutching his flashlight and pistol to his chest. The barrel was pointed at his chin. "Considering Roy's reputation, I knew everyone would believe he had run off with some woman. My secret would be safe." Elliott ceased rocking and moved his flashlight beam between Harry and me. "Until those two started snooping around."

Sheriff Hobart made a noble effort to divert Elliott's attention to him. "So . . . when Katherine discovered where you buried Roy, you moved his body here."

"I planned to bury Roy under the floor after the sale of the property was final. I thought this place would be leveled when the developers took over, and Roy's body would never be found."

Despite my fear, my curiosity begged to be satisfied. "Did you run Pudd Gormley off the road the other night?" I asked.

Elliott's tears stopped, and he looked at me incredulously. "I had to. I saw Pudd talking to you and Templeton at the country club last Saturday. Since Sheriff Hobart didn't question me immediately, I assumed Pudd hadn't told you he had picked me up along Route 15 the night I dumped Roy's Jaguar in the park. Old no-load-on-the-circuit Pudd didn't have a clue what I was doing on that road, and didn't ask. But I couldn't chance Pudd telling you about it because I realized you and your partner would piece it together."

"I take it you also sent me that funeral arrangement." I persisted. Elliott nodded. I felt satisfied that I had correctly identified Elliott's handwriting. Clues I had been envisioning and hearing suddenly began flooding my mind. The saws—Elliott was a woodworker. The first time I had seen him, he had bragged about making his gun cabinet. The bells—he lived on Chapelbell Court. His fiancée paints porcelain bells.

"I tried to deter you, Katherine," Elliott growled, "but you wouldn't let it go."

Elliott and I looked at each other. He kept his pistol aimed at me while he knelt and unscrewed the cap on the gasoline can. He threw the cap at me, but it missed and bounced off the wall, hitting a stack of plastic serving trays with an unnerving clang. Elliott lifted the gasoline can.

Sheriff Hobart shouted, "Elliott, don't do it!"

Elliott cackled as he poured some of the gasoline onto the floor in front of him then stood and splashed the remainder over the equipment around me. A few drops dampened my pants.

Elliott removed a gold lighter from his pants pocket and flicked it on. "Roy gave me this monogrammed pipe lighter when I expressed an interest in pipe smoking." He stared at it. Perhaps he was remembering his happy times with Roy. Perhaps he was remembering murdering Roy.

Harry inched into the kitchen. However, Elliott caught sight of Harry's subtle movements as he was about to pass behind the sheriff. "Stay where you are Templeton! I know I am going to die in here . . . but I am not going to die alone. Your niece, Katherine,—that's a laugh—is going to die with me." Before anyone could move, Elliott tossed the lighter into the gasoline.

Flames shot up like a vaporous, golden screen between Elliott and me, casting a lurid light over this unlikely tomb. I felt trapped at the molten core of Elliott Danforth's emotional volcano. Perspiration began to pour down my face. Fearing Elliott would shoot at any movement, I was afraid to raise my hand to wipe it.

Harry moved slowly toward Elliott as Sheriff Hobart motioned for me to come to him. The heat was intense; black smoke billowed out both open doors. I could barely hear above the fire's roar. To attempt to draw Elliott's attention away from me, Harry shouted, "Elliott . . . you know Roy wasn't dead when you buried him."

"You are a liar, Templeton! Elliott shouted, his eyes wild as he took aim at Harry. Elliott looked like a cornered beast. But unlike a beast, his greed alone had brought this upon him. I stole several steps toward the sheriff.

Harry continued his attack, "It's true, Elliott. Roy was unconscious when you covered him with that damp earth."

Elliott noticed my attempted escape. Again, I became his target. Harry shouted, "You could have saved Roy if you had gotten him help."

"Shut up!!" Elliott screamed at Harry in desperation. "You are confusing me!" Elliott dropped his flashlight and gripped his pistol with both his shaking hands.

I had moved far enough away from Elliott to be one short step from Harry. Elliott raised his pistol and aimed directly at my chest. He shrieked, "All of this is your fault Katherine."

Harry lunged in front of me as Elliott pulled the trigger. In that instant, I thought I heard two shots. For what seemed an eternity, I felt suspended in time. When I finally moved, I raised my hands slowly to wipe the wetness from my face.

I lowered my hands and stared at them in paralyzing disbelief. My face was spattered with Harry's blood.

The ambulances carrying Harry and Elliott rode in tandem, their wailing sirens piercing the heavy night air. I sat on the emergency vehicle's steel floor alone . . . too far from Harry. He was surrounded by paramedics and basic life support personnel. I craned my neck to look between the jumble of lightning-quick, uniformed, legs and arms. Harry's blood gushed from the gauze bandages covering his naked chest. A clear plastic sealant resembling Handi Wrap was tapped over the scarlet gauze. IV's were attached to each arm. The monitors attached to his chest by ten fibrous leads reduced Harry's heartbeat to rhythmic, mechanical beeps.

I remember thinking the ride was too bumpy for Harry, and I asked someone who bent down to see if I was all right to tell the driver to be more careful. I needed to tell someone to do something.

During our lunch the previous Wednesday, Harry had finally convinced me I should view my visions as a way to help humanity, not as an embarrassing burden. I believed I could bring closure to Roy Allnutt's family by exposing his murderer. But at what price? Harry's life? That was too high a price to pay.

I am a spiritual but not a particularly religious person. But I folded my sooty hands and prayed.

"Dear God, I know I have no right to ask for favors. You know better than anyone that I am undeserving. But, please, please don't let Harry Templeton die. I did not mean all those things I said about wanting him to go away. Well . . . I did at first; but the longer I knew him, the more I realized what a truly good man he is. Please God . . . if you need to take something, take it from me. Take my money. Take my career. But . . . please God . . . I'm begging you, do not take Harry Templeton's life."

One of the paramedics walked over and warned that if I

wanted to spend time with Harry, I should do it now. I rose and hurried to Harry's side. I took his hands in mine. His hands were cold. As Harry opened his eyes and looked up at me, I tried to suppress my tears. I bent over Harry. The smell of antiseptic mingled with the smell of smoke. I wished the smell had been of Harry's cigars. My tears fell on his face, and I wiped them gently with my fingers. He tried several times to speak, but each time he coughed violently.

"Don't try to talk now, Harry, we will have plenty of time later." I attempted a smile. "I know you did not mean all those nasty things you said to me on the phone tonight. You wanted to keep me from pursuing Roy's murderer. You were trying to keep me safe." I gave his hand a squeeze of thanks. "Elliott said that you and I are partners. And that is what we are, Harry. We are partners." I choked back a sob.

Harry's breathing appeared labored. Still holding Harry's hand, I straightened up and motioned for the paramedics. They adjusted the leads to the monitors and checked his chest with a stethoscope. I would not relinquish Harry's hand—I remained by his side.

Harry stared at me blankly for what seemed like forever. Eventually, Harry again attempted to speak. I knelt beside Harry and put my face close to his. Harry blinked several times and whispered, "Kate, my beauty, please take care of Hathaway."

Epilogue

The day after the shooting, Ric went to Harry's apartment, collected Hathaway's things, and took Harry's cat home with him. Ric volunteered to look after Hathaway until I could devote the time to him we knew he would require. After all, Harry had asked me to take care of his beloved pet, and that was what I intended to do.

I told my partners an emergency had arisen and I needed to take a short-term leave of absence. I did not elaborate, and they did not question me. Because I had not missed a day at the office since my dad's funeral, the firm's partners knew that the emergency must have been serious. Quite frankly, at that point, I cared little what my partners thought.

As much as the medical staff would allow, I remained at Harry's bedside in the Intensive Care Unit. My housekeeper took care of my pets. Elliott's bullet had pierced Harry's lung and collapsed it. For the first week, Harry's hold on life was tenuous. I sat alone in Harry's sterile hospital room consoled only by the monitors attached to his motionless body. With each peak and valley that registered on the screens and each audible "blip" that emanated from some hidden mechanical device, I became acutely aware of our dependence on technology. Those machines were keeping Harry alive. They were the only indicators that Harry was, in fact, alive. As I sat silently with Harry, I ultimately questioned what it meant to be alive. If life was defined as a seemingly mechanical, redundant process, then I was alive. However, if life was defined as a spontaneous, glorious adventure, then I was not alive. I felt an unnerving empathy with Harry's condition. I prayed that Harry's was only temporary. I wondered if I could alter mine.

The second week, Harry's prognosis improved. He began to recognize me, speak, and sit up in bed. By the third week, Harry's doctors were predicting a full recovery. I was elated. Harry asked when he could smoke one of the cigars he found in the fruit basket Ric sent. His doctors and I answered a resounding "Never!"

Elliott Danforth had not been as fortunate as Harry. He died in the ambulance on the way to the hospital. During one of Rowena's visits to Harry, she confessed to being emotionally torn. She felt hatred toward Elliott for murdering her father, but she still felt some strange loyalty toward him as the man she had agreed to marry. Rowena commented that considering Elliott's personality, she was convinced Elliott would rather have died than spend one day of his life in a prison cell. I agreed.

Both Roy and Elliott were buried in the Montaview Memorial Cemetery. I found it ironic that the Allnutt and Danforth family graves were adjacent to one another. The tip of Elliott's grave touched the tip of Roy's. Someone had said that since the first time they had met, Elliott Danforth aspired to be like Roy Allnutt. On some subconscious level hidden beneath Elliott's pompous, yet insecure facade, I believed Roy's death would have left an incredible void in Elliott's life.

Victor and Marjorie visited Harry religiously. One day Victor announced he had found evidence amongst some long-forgotten family papers that their home had been used as a Civil War hospital. Victor had presented those papers to the local historical society and found that, as owners, his family was eligible for federal monies to restore the farm to its original state. Marjorie added that the family was going to turn the farm into a nursery . . . after Victor and she returned from their honeymoon, of course.

Mark busied himself planning the nursery layout. But he did find the time to visit Harry often. One day, Mark walked into Harry's room with two bouquets of flowers from his gardens. Mark arranged the one bouquet in a vase on Harry's window sill. The other bouquet Mark handed to me.

About The Author

Deborah Heinecker hails from Baltimore, Maryland. She is the only child of doting parents, Calvin and Lorraine Heinecker. However, Deborah contends she was only slightly spoiled. Deborah holds a BA in English with an emphasis on medieval literature from the University of Maryland at Baltimore County. She minored in Accounting.

Deborah's first position after graduation was with the Treasury Department as a National Bank Examiner. After several months, Deborah realized accounting was not her cup of tea. She combined her computer knowledge with her writing abilities and became a consultant developing standards and user manuals for corporate clients.

Deborah enjoys horseback riding, tennis, sailing, and the symphony. She has studied classical ballet, homeopathy, Reiki and other healing modalities.

Since her unlikely career move from businesswoman to psychic detective, Deborah has assisted with 46 criminal cases nationwide. She was the subject of Channel 9's series *Visions of Crime* and has been the focus of various magazine and news articles. Deborah recently took a sabbatical to write her first mystery. It was developed as a series featuring her reluctant psychic detective, Katherine St. George, and is based on one of her early cases. Deborah is currently working on the second mystery of the series.

Deborah is married to poet, Bob Wickless. They reside in a turn-of-the-century Victorian in northern Frederick County with their canine and feline motley crew.